Passing

THROUGH THE FIRE

THE METHUSELAH CHRONICLES
-BOOK TWO-

T. B. Thornton, Th.M.

Printed in the United States of America

Publishing services by Selah Publishing Group, LLC, Tennessee. The views expressed or implied in this work do not necessarily reflect those of Selah Publishing Group.

ISBN: 978-1-58930-324-9
Library of Congress Control Number: 2023907592

Dedication

This book is dedicated to my parents, Jim and Barbara Thornton. Admittedly, I was not an easy child to raise! I have been very blessed to have two wonderful examples of God's love to guide me. They continue to be my greatest fans and, without them and their constant prayers over my life, I don't know where I would have ended up. Thank you Mom and Dad!

Foreword

The story within the pages of this book, though purely fictional, illustrates the extent to which Satan's lies can permeate man's thinking and man's ability to see what he believes, even if those beliefs are false. Make no mistake, Satan is *very* good at what he does! He is, after all, the "father of lies." However, those lies can only affect our reality if we give ourselves over to them, thereby deputizing Satan and giving him the authority to shape what we see.

More importantly, this story will also illustrate God's ability to reach down into those false realities and bring clarity of thought and sight to those who desire more than the empty promises of Satan. I pray that my readers will learn the depths of God's love for them, the extent to which He will go to draw them back to Himself, and the redemption available through His Son, Jesus Christ. Through the acceptance of Jesus as the Perfect Lamb of Sacrifice and the indwelling of the Holy Spirit within, we are better able to reject Satan's lies and live a life of victory over his demonic influences.

— T. B. Thornton, Th.M

Chapter 1

Years since creation; 636

THE VERY EDGE OF THE SUN COULD BE SEEN PEEKING over the rim of the low mountain range across the expansive valley from where fourteen-year-old Enoch stood atop the high hills. An oddly chill wind was flowing up the hillside and wafting through his hair as young Enoch stared down into the valley, eyeing the small city and villages that lined the river which meandered its way through the basin. Strangely, although a long way off, he could hear the sounds of carefree frivolity emanating from them as the inhabitants laughed, hollered, yelled, and cavorted in their wine-fueled orgies of sin and vice.

Enoch had no personal knowledge of who these people were but had a strong sense of what they had become. They had turned *from* God *toward* the god of self, believing in nothing more than the moment at hand and the good feeling given them by the grape and the grope of anyone willing to debase themselves in kind. His heart felt sorrow for the wasted lives being led by these poor, deceived people. He was astonished at the ease with which they had turned from their purpose to this haphazard existence they were now embracing.

A distant rumble from somewhere within the earth jarred him from his thoughts. The sky started to turn an ominous green and black as it began to boil, swirling and flashing with brilliant reddish-gold illuminations. His heart sank within his chest at the sight of it as a fearsome awe swept over him that he had never experienced in his young life. He wondered what all this could mean as his soul cried out silently to God.

Without warning, an ear-splitting explosion erupted in the distance. Enoch's eyes found the source of the disturbance, but his mind had trouble deciphering what he was witnessing. It looked as if a great fountain was spewing up from the earth and climbing ever higher into the darkening sky until it seemed to punch a hole into the upper limits of the firmament. He watched as the fountain grew wider and elongated, following the course of the river, surging and cascading its way ever closer to the unsuspecting townships in the valley.

Then, as his mind tried vainly to make sense of all he saw, twisted tree branches, large pebbles, small stones, and showers of soil and water started raining down around him. He thought it strange that he wasn't worried for his own safety as much as for the desperate souls in the valley, who he could now hear crying out to the Creator, begging for a savior to deliver them from certain death. But it was already too late. The catastrophic explosions of raging groundwater were upon them, obliterating everything and everyone without prejudice.

Following close behind was a quickly rising torrent of flood waters, filling the valley from one end to the other. The muddy liquid surged so rapidly and violently that nothing could stand in its way. Huge trees were snapped off like dry twigs, and colossal boulders were washed violently out of place as if they were feathers.

Enoch's heart felt as if it would burst in his chest from the pure terror of what he was witnessing. The waters were rising up, up, racing up the hillside, threatening to swallow him! He screamed out in horror!

"Oh, God, please save them!"

———◦/◦/◦———

"Oh, God, please save them!" Enoch awoke with a start, sitting straight up in bed. He was covered in sweat, chest heaving, eyes darting around, and mouth dry. He instinctively looked to the floor, expecting to see the water rushing up to swallow him, but he could see none in the early morning sunlight that was just starting to ease its way through the window.

Realizing finally that he had been dreaming, he tried to slow his breathing and calm his nerves. With trembling hands, he wiped the sweat from his face, collapsed onto the bed, and stared at the ceiling. His mind slowly eased him back to reality. He was in a room in the home of his grandfather, Mahalalel, where he had been helping him with his harvest. He seemed to be safe, and the world outside wasn't exploding. However, he wanted to be sure.

He jumped out of bed and hurried through the quiet house toward the door. When he reached it, he eased it open and, with that wary feeling in his heart, peered out into the world. To his relief, all seemed normal as the early morning mists sailed across the expansive lawn. Birds were singing their praises to the new day, the behemoths were bellowing to each other at the opposite side of the small dell where they were having a breakfast of cypress leaves, and the sky was the correct shade of pastel blue and not crashing down upon him. He was finally at ease and felt relieved and safe.

In his young life, he had never had a dream as real or as terrible as the one he had awakened to. He knew he would never forget it. He also felt as though he was not supposed to forget it. He walked out onto the lawn, knelt where he was, and prayed to the Creator, thanking God for entrusting him with the vision, even one with such a tragic outcome. He would just have to trust the Lord to reveal its purpose when He was ready.

Chapter 2

Years since creation; 708

A NALEAH SANG QUIETLY AND SOOTHINGLY WITH a quivering voice as she was pushed along the dusty street toward the city furnace. She wiped the tears from the head of her one-year-old son, Joaz, as they streamed down her face and onto his. Though she had known this horrible event was coming for many days now, she had hoped that somehow it wouldn't. She hoped that her husband, Jotham, would come to his senses, gather his family, and escape this cruel and evil city. But, alas, here she was, taking this awful walk to the place where her nightmares would begin.

To avoid the thought of what was happening, she allowed her mind to wander back to a happier time when she and Jotham were first married and had just moved to the quaint little city of Baalta from a small village up the valley. They were looking forward to their future with such high hopes. They had planned to raise a family and build a good life together. Jotham was going to open a bakery in the city, supplied with wheat from her family's farm back in the village. She would help him and raise strong children who would eventually grow up to find happiness the way the two of them had. It all seemed so clear then. She knew that some troubles would come, but together they could overcome whatever challenges came their way.

Now, however, she realized that that future—that fantasy—would never come true. Those thoughts from the past now seemed like childish, romantic dreams that were about to go up in the black, putrid smoke of the city's furnace. Her new reality was a dismal life where happiness had no part.

Preoccupied with her thoughts, she was barely aware that Jotham had placed a gentle hand on her shoulder as he spoke reassuringly, "Analeah, I know you are upset. I, too, wish there was another way, but Simyaza says we must do this if we are to be successful and prosper. We must do as he says. He requires this of us if we are to gain his blessings."

She looked back at him and was sickened by the sight. She was sickened by the very sound of his voice over the past few days. This man, who looked so much like the man she had married, had been replaced by someone she didn't know. In place of the Jotham, who was happy, strong, and loving, there was now a miserable, weak, and sycophantic imposter. She had already decided that she would never love him again. The place inside her where that love had once lived was now empty, hard, and black. She cared no more for herself. She loved no one but her son. For this reason, she had decided that this world was too cruel for such a beautiful soul to be forced to live. This was the only thing that kept her moving along toward her destination.

As she rounded the final corner, she was blasted in the face with the odor of evil. She was stricken with a sense of conviction as she neared the steps that led to the top. She decided within herself, "This is what my own soul must smell like. This is the smell of my guilt."

As the unhappy family reached the furnace and climbed the staircase that led to the peak, she looked directly into the black eyes of Simyaza, who smiled down at her benevolently as if he were going to do her a favor. "Analeah, I know this is hard for you and Jotham, but I assure you, this will be for the best. I have to know that you are willing to do anything I ask of you if I am to shower you with my blessings."

With that, he reached out his arms and wrapped his long, boney fingers around Joaz's arm and leg. He held them there, not pulling him away; only waiting until the child was given over. The final decision had to be made by the parents. Simyaza could only entice them with his promises.

Analeah looked down into her son's eyes one final time and kissed him on the forehead. She wanted the moment to go on a little longer, but she saw Jotham reaching out to touch him and shoved Joaz quickly into the arms of Simyaza so that she could at least cheat Jotham out of that one final pleasure.

Simyaza grinned ravenously at the child and then turned to the waiting crowd below. "Of all the people on the earth, my master has chosen to bless you, the people of this valley, first. When the stories of Enoch, the man of Urna who claims to speak to God, reached you, many of you were led astray and started to turn to his false doctrines. This angered my master, the *true* god. In his anger, he gave me the power over all the livestock and crops of this valley to show you his displeasure over your blasphemies. I followed his directives and made your livestock sickly and frail. I caused your crops to wither and die, even with an abundance of water to nourish them. My master wanted to teach you that you are all cursed without him.

"Since then, you have all felt the effects of his curse. You have felt hunger, your businesses have failed, and your economy has stagnated. This used to be a lush valley full of happy and contented people, but your decision to follow the teachings of that false profit from Urna has only led to your demise.

"However, in his mercy, my master has seen fit to give you the opportunity to redeem yourselves and gain his graces once more. All he asks is that you show your faith with an act of sacrifice *worthy* of that grace. Those of you who have chosen to turn to my master and make that sacrifice have seen your crops come back to life, even while the crops of your neighbors continue to fail. You have seen your livestock gain strength and prosper, while the livestock of your neighbors remain sick and die. He has proven himself to you in every case. Yet, some of you still choose to defy him."

Simyaza turned and pointed back at Jotham, "Jotham was, until today, one of you. But he has chosen to turn back to my master, the true god, and make the show of faith that my master requires. He has chosen a life of plenty over a life of starvation. He has chosen to give his family a chance at success rather than a future of failure.

"I am sure that his decision was a hard one. What my master asks is much. But if you genuinely care for your family and their future, as Jotham obviously does, there is no other choice you can make.

"Jotham and his wife, Analeah, have willingly handed over this fine son, Joaz, to my master so that they will again please him and regain the grace that was once theirs."

Simyaza then walked to the edge of the furnace opening and held Joaz by one leg, dangling him over the gaping mouth as the black smoke billowed, swallowing up the small form. Feeling the intense heat, Joaz let out a shrill scream and cried for his mother, who was now on her knees looking on in horror.

Simyaza now closed his eyes and spoke loudly with a prayerful cadence, "I commit this child to you, my master, the true god of this earth, and ask for your blessings to now fall onto the family of Jotham, your faithful servant."

With that, he let go of the screaming child. Joaz disappeared into the fiery abyss, and a puff of coal-black smoke blew back out to mark his ghastly reception.

The ghoulish crowd of Simyaza's followers let out a cheer as Analeah fell limp and howled in instant remorse for the thing she had done.

Chapter 3

*M*ETHUSELAH AND HIS COUSIN, JUBAL, WATCHED nervously as their colossal friend placed the final portion of the roof gently upon the log frame of the house. If his measurements were correct, it would slip snuggly down into place and look as if the entire roof was one piece. Gardan lowered it slowly until it rested at a slight tilt, hung up on one corner. Methuselah's heart sank a bit at the sight as his mind raced to figure out where his calculations had gone wrong. "How far off was I, Gardan?" he asked, looking up at the giant man.

Gardan stooped down to look closely at the point of trouble, then stood and smiled at his young friend, "Not as far as you think, my friend." He then lightly bumped the edge of the roof piece with the heel of his palm, and, with a thud, the section fell tightly into place.

"Yes!" hollered the two cousins with their fists raised high in the air, signifying victory. Neither of the two young men had ever embarked on a building project of this magnitude in their relatively short lives, and the accomplishment felt good.

Even if they wanted to, Methuselah and Jubal could not deny their family relation. Jubal had dirty blonde hair and deep

17

brown eyes. In contrast, Methuselah had wavy, raven-colored hair with bright blue eyes and was slightly taller at just over four cubits. However, they were both ruggedly built with the same square jawlines. They were born just days apart and grew up in adjoining valleys doing the same farm work at young ages. Now, at twenty-four, they were exceedingly strong and solidly firm in their work ethics.

More important than any of this was the other family trait they had inherited from their fathers; their unwavering faith in the Creator. This had shaped their lives and formed their character more than anything else. For every good thing, they would thank God. And for every hardship, they would seek God's perfect will and loving guidance to bring them through.

As Methuselah stood looking at his new home, he quietly praised the Creator for this latest blessing.

"Methuselah," said Gardan looking down at the nearly finished house. "I believe this will make a fine home for you and your new bride."

Methuselah eyed the structure with satisfaction and nodded, "Yes, I believe it will. All we need to do now is to put the doors on and move in the furnishings."

"We should be able to get that done today," said Jubal. "I think Tamari will be happy with her new home. Don't you?"

"Yes, I think she will," a female voice behind them said. The two men turned quickly to see the young women approaching. Their hearts melted anew as they always seemed to at the sight of Tamari and her sister, Julis, as they neared.

Julis was one year younger than Tamari at the age of twenty-three. She was almost four cubits tall—a bit taller than Tamari—with a slender build. Her naturally curly, dark brown hair flowed gently over her shoulders, framing her delicate facial features and large hazel eyes. Her carefree disposition and easy smile made her all the more attractive to Jubal, who had been hopelessly in love with her for as long as he could remember.

Tamari, on the other hand, had a softer, shapelier build. Her long, sandy-blonde hair also had a natural curl but framed a face with an effortless, classic beauty. She had a more serious disposition than her sister. Still, she also had a mischievous, fun-loving way about her that could be easily seen in the twinkle of her bright green eyes.

Methuselah had known since the age of eight that she would one day be his wife, and as she approached him now, his heart nearly leaped out of his chest at the thought of their wedding, which was only days away. He bounded the space between them. Knowing what was coming, Tamari quickly dropped the basket she was carrying just in time as he wrapped his muscular arms around her, picking her up and spinning her around, delighting in the sound of her girlish squeals of delight.

"Put me down, you brute!" she mockingly scolded him. "Who do you think you are that you can attack me this way?"

He put her down and backed away slightly, bowing deeply with a gallant flourish of his hand, "My apologies dear lady, as I seem to have temporarily lost control of my senses at the sight of your striking beauty." He then looked up at her and smiled teasingly. "However, once I have trapped you in marriage, you will be defenseless against my attacks."

"Is that what you think?" asked Tamari with her hands on her hips. She playfully shook her head. "We will see. Perhaps I will have to head you off with a surprise attack of my own." Methuselah feigned a look of terror and turned slightly away as if frightened at the thought.

Jubal finally had to cut in and put a stop to their little performance, "Would you two please give us a break from your disgusting gushing over each other? We all know you are hopelessly in love." He waved a hand toward Julis, who stood beside him, "I am in love with Julis too, but do you see me gushing over *her* like that?"

He looked at Julis and, instead of getting the agreement he thought he would, he was getting a harsh stare from beneath raised eyebrows. He instantly realized his blunder and tried vainly to recover, "Well…uh…You know what I mean…uh… Those two just take it so far. They…"

Julis sympathetically held up her hand, stopping him from digging deeper, "I know what you meant, Jubal. It *can* be a bit sickening how they act at times, but a *little* of that wouldn't kill you." Jubal opened his mouth as if he wanted to reply but thought better of it and closed it again.

Gardan, who had been watching the entire comedy play out before him, had to let out a deep-throated chuckle. Then, noticing the look Jubal shot at him, he busied himself by fidgeting with the roof section again. He couldn't help but smile at how his young friends interacted with each other. He also couldn't help but feel blessed by the companionship of these people he considered family.

Many years ago, the only family he had was his father, Azazel, and his brothers, six of whom he had lived with in a hidden compound atop a secluded mountain far to the northeast. All that was left of those times were the painful memories of what those days were like for him.

His father, Azazel, was an angel of God who had turned his back on the Creator to follow Lucifer in the great rebellion in Heaven. Lucifer had put Azazel in charge of corrupting the bloodlines of the humans and teaching them how to make war with each other. To that end, he had shown the humans how to make swords and shields and turned them against each other, selling them on the idea that they could have whatever they wanted, even if it meant killing each other to get it. In return for his "services," he only asked that he be given a wife from among the women in the cities he was "serving."

This unholy union between him, a "son of God," and the human women led to the birth of giants, of which Gardan was one of twenty-two such children. Sixteen of these children had grown to be so violent and uncontrollable that Azazel was forced to send them away far to the north. Their father trained the remaining six in the cruel art of destruction, only to be released upon the world to wreak havoc when Azazel felt the time was right. At a height three times that of humans, and ten times their strength, the fury released upon the unsuspecting people would indeed be awesome.

Gardan had always abhorred the violence and cruelty of his father and brothers. He instead preferred the company of the forest animals with which he had an uncanny ability to communicate and befriend. This perceived weakness made him an easy target for ridicule at the hands of his evil father and siblings. He struggled for many years to find his place in the freakish society into which he was born and consigned himself to stay and look after his mother, who was treated with equal cruelty.

One day, Gardan's brother, an ignorant and violent single-eyed giant named Syclah, went into a rage about something and killed Gardan's mother. He was understandably stricken with grief over it, but Azazel and his brothers merely mocked him for his emotional softness. However, instead of breaking his will, Gardan became more defiant of his father and attempted to kill him. But, he was blind-sided, beaten nearly to death, and left for dead.

However, the Creator knew Gardan's heart and decided to take what Azazel meant for evil and use it for His good. Through His providence, Gardan was found by Methuselah's father, Enoch, and nursed back to health. In so doing, a friendship was formed that would eventually facilitate Gardan's coming to find faith in the Creator and healing his heart of the hatred he had been taught toward man. Looking down at his young friends now, he only felt love and loyalty toward them and thanked the Creator for choosing to show such favor upon him.

"Is anyone hungry?" asked Tamari as she began to unload the basket she had brought. "I have lots of fruit and bread."

Methuselah looked at the bread warily, "Who made the bread?"

Tamari defensively put her hands on her hips and leveled her eyes at him, "I made the bread just the way your mother showed me! If you don't want any, you don't have to eat it. Then, there will be more for the rest of us."

Methuselah picked up one of the slightly misshapen loaves, inspecting it carefully, thumping the hard crust, and turning it over to reveal the black, clearly over-cooked bottom. "This looks much better than the last time."

She snatched it out of his hand and turned it back over to hide the burnt side again, a bit embarrassed, "Before you go complaining about it, just try it!" Then, with some difficulty, she tore a small piece off of the top of the loaf and handed it to him.

He took a bite and acted pleasantly surprised at how good it was, "Hey, this is pretty good! You *are* getting better, Sweetheart." The bread was dry and a little bitter, but it *was* an improvement over her last attempt. He chose to eat it without complaint to save her feelings. He only hoped the others would follow his lead and do the same.

The group gathered around and bowed their heads, giving thanks for their meal, their blessings, and their friendship before eating. Gardan, who had brought his own supply of food, sat down and joined them. He placed large bushels of fresh beans and several melons down and began to devour them. They all ate, laughing and enjoying each other's company as they spoke excitedly about the near future and the journey they were to take together to the Royal City in the next few days.

Chapter 4

*A*NALEAH STEALTHILY MADE HER WAY THROUGH the house, toward the door, carefully carrying her sleeping one-year-old little boy, Asham, in one arm. In the other arm, she carried a clean set of clothes for Asham and a small disk-shaped loaf of bread she had managed to hide away. Dangling from her fingertips were her sandals. She was afraid they would make too much noise and wake her husband before she could escape.

Before getting Asham from his bed, she had quietly cracked the front door open slightly so she wouldn't have to fumble with it while her arms were full. Then, after retrieving the small boy, she made her way back through the house toward the door. She easily pushed her way through and turned to close it by gently using her hip, careful not to let it close too loudly. She decided to leave it slightly ajar. As far as she and her son were concerned, it wouldn't matter anyway. They would never be back again.

Outside, in the blackness of the night, she took a slow, deep breath to steady her nerves for the next step of her escape from this hellish little city of Baalta. She looked warily down the narrow street in both directions to ensure no one else was around. Satisfied that they were alone, she slipped on her sandals and made her way from one shadow to the next.

Stopping at the intersection of her street and the main thoroughfare that led into and out of the city, she peered around the corner to see if any sentries were posted at the city gates. There appeared to be only one, but he seemed to be wide awake and at full attention. Her heart sank within her chest. "How am I going to get out of the city now?" she asked herself. Suddenly aware of how poorly she had planned her escape, tears started forming in the corners of her eyes.

She was a young woman of forty-three who had lived a good life in a small village on the outskirts of town until she married her husband ten years before. However, the last three years had been nothing more than a nightmare full of sorrows and guilt. Until she became pregnant with Asham, she had no longer cared for her husband or herself and had often contemplated suicide as a means of ending the dismal existence that was her lot in life. But now she felt she could give her new son what she had denied to Joaz. To do that, she had to get away from her husband, Baalta, and the city's governor, Simyaza.

It was true that since that darkest of days three years ago, their business had flourished, and their finances had improved dramatically. But it was all so empty and futile. She would gladly trade every so-called "blessing" of Simyaza for the life of her precious Joaz. She would relish the chance to feel the pangs of hunger rather than the coldness of her soul.

Tragically, though, she would have to live with the terrible choices of the past and devote herself to giving her new son a better life away from this city of evil. She hated the thought of what remaining here would mean, and she desperately needed to find another way out of the city.

A thought invaded her mind as if it came from outside herself: "Go out through the livestock gate." It was almost as if someone had whispered it to her. So much so that she turned quickly from side to side to see if anyone else was there. No, she was alone. Her heart lightened with the idea, "I never thought about it before. The livestock gate is never guarded like the main gate is!" A smile almost came to her face as she started making her way toward her new escape route.

Then, another thought entered her mind, "I'll have to go by the furnace to get there." Her stomach turned, and her mouth watered in preparation for the expulsion of her last meal. She scolded herself, breathing slowly to steady her nerves again, "I will do what I must do! Then, I will never have to see that horrible thing again. That furnace has taken enough from me! I refuse to allow it to stop me now!" She picked up her pace and made her way quickly through the alleyways in the less popu-lated part of the city that led to the livestock gates.

She didn't even look to her left as she passed by the fur-nace. She looked straight ahead and tried to hold her breath as long as she could to keep herself from taking in the disgusting stench of this place. Finally, she got past it and could see the livestock gate ahead of her.

The smell of animal dung was a welcome reprieve from the smell of the furnace. In a strange way, it was like a home-coming for her. It reminded her of simpler times in that small village where she grew up. The small gate, surrounded by a mixture of hay, mud, and feces, beckoned to her. She had to fight the urge to run through it as new tears began to stream down her cheeks—tears of happiness. They were welcomed tears, like friends she hadn't seen in a long time. She passed through the gate and quickly disappeared, enveloped by the darkness beyond.

—⁂—

Mirah tried to stifle her giggles as she waved the feather un-der Methuselah's nose. His eleven-year-old little sister loved to play tricks on her brother and, having been told to wake him up this morning gave her a chance she couldn't resist. After all, her mother hadn't specified *how* she was to wake him up.

She wiggled the feather gently, then backed off to a safe distance. Nothing. She wiggled it again. He stirred slightly and rubbed his nose before nestling in again. She wiggled it again and backed off. She again didn't get a reaction and decided she would have to be a little braver if she wanted to get the desired response. She tiptoed up next to the bed, held the feather right over his face, and brought it down toward his nose again. She was determined that she would tickle him awake with this feather if she had to shove it up his nose to do it.

Methuselah suddenly opened his eyes wide and yelled, "AHA!" Mirah jumped a cubit into the air and screamed, dropping the feather right where it was as he reached out and grabbed her belly. She squealed and ran through the door, hiding behind her mother, who was alerted by all the commotion.

"What are you two up to?" Ednah asked with her hands on her hips.

Mirah threw her hands up as if to show herself innocent of any wrongdoing, "I was just doing as I was told. I woke him up like you asked."

Methuselah picked the feather up off the floor and stood with it held up in front of him, "Mother, is this what you told her to wake me up with?"

Ednah smirked a bit as she turned to see the guilty face of her daughter. Mirah pleaded with her eyes for her mother to play along. Ednah turned back to Methuselah and shrugged her shoulders, "Methuselah, I thought you liked to be woken up gently. What could be gentler than a feather?"

His eyes narrowed as he looked incredulously past his mother at the wide grin of his little sister. She was obviously taking great delight in her small victory. He then looked back to his mother, shaking his head, "I see that I'm outnumbered this morning. Where is Father? Perhaps he will help me even the score."

Mirah put her hands on her hips, cocking her head to one side to add emphasis, "He is out watching the fish on his bench by the stream, but *he's* going to take my side too!"

"Not if I get to him first!" said Methuselah bolting toward the door.

Surprised, Mirah squealed and turned to run. The chase was on, and she had a head start. She ran as fast as her skinny legs could take her toward the door of the house, scrambling to open it and get out the door before Methuselah could make up the ground. But, as she got it open, he slid by her in a flash and was out in the yard, rounding the house toward the stream.

At this point, he decided to tease her. He turned around and asked her with a snicker, "Why are you so slow? Is it because you run like a girl?"

Mirah attempted to run around him, but he blocked her way, moving from side to side. "I *am* a girl!" she yelled as she gave him a wimpy punch in the arm.

Methuselah grabbed the spot on his arm where she had punched him and feigned severe pain as he let out a howl, "Oh! The pain!" Then he let her run around him and win the little race.

Enoch, who had heard all this commotion, had turned and was watching the proceedings with an amused look on his face. He loved seeing these two interact this way and delighted in the love they showed through their play. He had to laugh a bit when Mirah finally arrived, a little disheveled and out of breath from the run.

"Mirah, is your brother being mean to you again?" asked Enoch with feigned worry and surprise.

"He's teasing me!" she said accusingly, pointing at him. "All I did was wake him up like Mother had asked, but he started chasing me."

Enoch's eyes widened knowingly, "And I know how much you hate being chased like that." Mirah nodded with overacted exaggeration. "I'll tell you what; you go back to the house and help your mother with the preparations for our trip, and I'll have a stern talk with that mean old brother of yours."

She smiled mischievously at Methuselah and marched victoriously past him. "Hmm!" she snorted with her nose in the air. Methuselah only shook his head and mussed her hair a bit.

Methuselah and Enoch exchanged a muffled laugh between them as Methuselah made his way to the bench where his father was sitting. Enoch watched as his son sat. He was so proud of the man Methuselah had become. He excitedly looked forward to the future he and Tamari would share.

Enoch turned his attention back to the little stream his bench overlooked. He loved to come and sit in this shady spot underneath the sprawling limbs of a massive cedar tree. The stream made a sudden bend around the tree and, as a result, was a bit wider and deeper here than in any other place. It made a perfect little nursery for the wide varieties of fish that made their lives in the labyrinth of waterways that meandered through Enoch's little valley. The streams watered his crops effortlessly, along with the myriad flowers and grasses that colorfully carpeted the scene around his home.

The sweet aromas of blossoms wafted unseen through the air, riding the gentle mists that perpetually drifted over the landscape. A cacophony of sounds was on display. The calls of a hundred species of birds and waterfowl seamlessly intertwined with the bellows of the behemoths that feed on the lower leaves of the three-hundred-cubit-tall cypress trees in the swampy end of the valley.

At this moment, however, Enoch was oblivious to all the beauty surrounding him. His thoughts were solely on his son. He took a deep breath before speaking. "I guess you will not have the time to sit here with your father like this after today, will you, Son?" he said as he gently patted Methuselah on the knee.

Methuselah smiled at him softly, shaking his head, "Father, you know that's not true. I will always have time to spend with you. You will need help with your crops when they come, and I will need help when mine come in next season. That is the way our family has always done things. Besides, I have a feeling I'm going to need your advice about…other things along the way." This last statement Methuselah made was accompanied by a distant, thoughtful stare out across the valley.

Enoch gave his son a moment, knowing the fears going through the young man's mind. They were the same fears that went through his mind many years before when he was about to start his new life with Ednah. He vividly remembered his own worries and had the same conversation with his father. He decided to save his son the awkwardness of asking the questions and voiced them for him, "Will I be a good husband to Tamari? Will I be able to provide for her? Will I, one day, be a good father to my own children?"

A bit surprised, Methuselah looked into his father's eyes with wonder, "Did the Lord tell you what my thoughts were?"

Enoch laughed deeply, "No, my son. He did not have to tell me. I was only repeating the questions I asked your grandfather before I married your mother."

Methuselah was taken aback by his father's answer, "You are a great husband to Mother, and have been a wonderful father to Mirah and me! Father, you are so wise where these things are concerned. How could you have had these same worries?"

Enoch slapped his son on the knee again with another laugh, "Methuselah, your mother was, and still is, the most beautiful creature I had ever seen. I was so in love with her that I didn't want to make any mistakes. I didn't want to do anything to disappoint her. I wanted to be the perfect husband.

I suspect that you have the same aspirations when it comes to your lovely Tamari, do you not?"

Methuselah nodded with excitement, feeling as if he had just heard his own jumbled thoughts put into words, "Yes, Father, that is exactly how I feel! I want everything to be perfect, just the way it is with you and Mother."

This statement elicited another hearty laugh from Enoch, "*Perfect?* My son, I hate to disappoint you, but 'perfect' would not be a word I would use to describe my life with your mother. Do not misunderstand. Your mother and I have had a wonderful marriage with memories I would never trade for anything this world offers. Still, there have also been some very trying times.

"For instance, you know how I tend to go on long walks with the Lord, sometimes not returning home for days." Methuselah nodded. "Well, it took your mother a long time to get used to that. I would walk in after being gone for a few days as if I had only stepped out for a moment. I expected her to welcome me home with open arms and set a meal before me while waiting patiently for me to regale her with my stories of adventure. I thought she should just understand that I was speaking with the Lord and spending time with Him. I thought that should be good enough and I wouldn't have to explain myself.

"Well, instead, what I got was a wife who felt neglected and lonely. Although it was true that I was spending that time with the Creator, I was also leaving her at home for days at a time, sometimes not even telling her when I left or giving her any idea how long I might be gone. The Lord came first in my life, as it should be. However, He also gave me a loving wife who, out of that love, was going to worry about me. The Lord helped me to understand that over time. My first priority is to the Creator, but my second priority is to your mother. The Creator wants us to spend time with Him, loving Him and worshiping

Him for all that He has blessed us with. But, He also expects us to show appreciation for those blessings by treating them with respect. By asking your mother to just accept my being gone for days with no notice or no idea how long I might be gone, I was mistreating the most wonderful blessing the Lord had ever given me."

Methuselah gave it some thought before speaking, "I guess I never thought about it too much. Growing up, it seemed normal to me that you went on your long walks. Mother would seem a bit lonely sometimes, walking out and staring up the valley, looking to see if you were coming, but she never seemed angry about it."

Enoch pursed his lips and nodded, "Do you know why I always come back with a beautiful flower to give her?" Methuselah only shook his head. "I do that to let her know I am thinking of her. Even though I am not with her, my thoughts are."

Methuselah took a deep breath and rested his face in his hands, "I have a lot to learn." It was quiet for a time before he spoke again, "Were there any other problems between you in the beginning?"

Enoch thought for a moment, "There weren't really any other problems that would amount to anything. There were a lot of adjustments I had to make, however."

"Adjustments?" Methuselah asked. "What kind of adjustments?"

Enoch smiled, "Well, I grew up with your grandmother's cooking." He looked over at his son as they exchanged knowing expressions and thoughts of the wonderful pies and treats that often came to the table in her house during their visits. Enoch continued, "Your mother's cooking is pretty good too, but it wasn't always that way."

It was now Methuselah's turn to give a good belly laugh, "Father, you should see the bread that Tamari has tried to bake! I feel so bad for her. She tries so hard, but it is simply terrible! She burns it so…"

"Methuselah!" His mother's voice scolded disapprovingly from behind them. "Tamari has been trying very hard to learn how to cook for you! You had better show some appreciation for that!"

Both men shot up from the bench, hands behind their backs as if they had been caught doing something naughty. Enoch fumbled with a response, "Ednah, we were…"

She cut him off, "I heard what you were saying. Your mother's cooking wasn't *that* good, you know." She finally smirked at the two of them standing there so helpless. She relented a bit, "If we're going to leave for the Royal City today, you two better get busy. There is still a lot to do." She paused momentarily before adding one more jab, "*If* you are interested, there is some food on the table for you. I hope it is to your liking!" With that, she turned and walked back to the house.

Father and son looked at each other again and chuckled before following.

Chapter 5

*J*OTHAM'S THOUGHTS WERE WHIRLING IN HIS MIND. He had awoken to find his wife and son gone, and his front door cracked open. He walked out and called her name, but to no avail. That alone didn't worry him much. She would often make an early morning trip to the small market in the town's square to get something she needed or to see a neighbor, but she had never left the door open like that. Pushing that thought aside, he decided she had probably just forgotten to close it, busy with an energetic Asham.

He dressed and headed out the door, taking the route Analeah would have followed toward the market. He soon met with Analeah's widowed friend, Noalah, as she returned home from that direction. Jotham stood in her path and smiled a toothy grin at her as she approached, "Greetings, Noalah. How are you this morning?"

Noalah's heart sank within her chest at the sight of him and at the sound of his voice. She did not like him. Not because of anything he had done to her personally but because of the torment he had put Analeah through in his attempts to gain favor with Simyaza. The two women had provided a shoulder of support for each other on many occasions. Noalah had been there for Analeah when Joaz was, at least in her eyes, murdered in the name of Jotham's prosperity. And Analeah was there for

Noalah when her own husband, Kanlon, who had decided to speak out against Simyaza and his evil edicts and policies, was mysteriously attacked by some unknown animals and killed.

To that point, no animal had ever purposefully attacked a person. However, at the gruesome discovery of Kanlon's body, it was apparent that something very powerful with very sharp teeth and claws had killed him. She had always suspected that Simyaza had something to do with it but had no way to prove it. Nor did she have anyone, at least in the Simyaza-friendly town of Baalta, who would believe her, except Analeah.

Noalah, swallowing her mistrust for the moment, stopped. She kept a respectful distance and answered curtly, "Jotham."

Jotham, recognizing the apparent dislike Noalah had for him, suspended any further formalities, "Have you been to the market this morning?"

She answered simply, "Yes."

"Did you happen to see my wife and son there?" Jotham asked.

"No," Noalah answered.

Jotham was tiring of Noalah's one-word answers, "Well, have you seen her at *all* this morning? Do you have any idea where she may be? She and Asham were gone when I woke up this morning."

Noalah fought the temptation of saying what she was thinking, *"I pray to God that she has left you and this accursed city forever!"* Instead, she answered him bluntly, "I have not spoken to her today and have no idea where she may be." With that, she quickly edged around him and continued on her way.

Jotham was a bit surprised at her shortness and barked out after her, "If you see her, tell her I am looking for her!" He watched for an acknowledgment of his request but got none. He turned, muttering under his breath, "Your husband probably *begged* those beasts to eat him just to get away from *you!*"

He then decided that he would make his own search of the market. "Even if Noalah *had* seen her, that hateful woman wouldn't tell me," he whispered to himself. However, after an exhaustive search and many inquiries of the townspeople, he came up empty-handed. He then went back home, assuming she had returned, only to find his house the way he had left it. Now, he began to worry.

He spent the rest of the day walking the small city's streets. The sky was darkening now, and his worries turned not to fear or concern but to anger and revenge for the embarrassment that would come his way when the townspeople found out that his wife had left him and taken his son. He had aspirations of becoming one of the city leaders, but this would open him up to ridicule from the other men of Baalta. He only had to look at recent examples to know how it would end.

Since the instatement of the sacrifices, other women had attempted to leave the city. They had all been caught in the act and were severely punished and beaten in the city square. If Simyaza decided this punishment was enough, the husbands could keep their wives. Still, those men were perceived to have lost control over their households and, thus, unfit for leadership. However, if the husband sacrificed his wife to Simyaza, he was seen to have made atonement for his wife's wrongdoing. He would, once again, be looked upon with favor for making such a sacrifice in the name of community cohesiveness.

Jotham was almost surprised at how quickly he deliberated the case in his mind, "Ever since we sacrificed Joaz, she has made my life miserable! She has blamed me for wanting only the best for our family. I told her that we could have another child. And I was right! I gave her Asham, but was that good enough? No! She still insisted on treating me with disdain. Why does she think she's better than me in any case? Did she not hand Joaz over to Simyaza herself? I have tried to overlook her disrespect long enough!" He clenched his fists as he continued down the street toward his newfound destination.

"Given the way she has treated me over the last three years, this may be the best thing that could have happened. When I find her, I will waste no time! If the choice is life with a hateful wife and the ridicule of the townspeople, or life as a city leader and the favor of Simyaza, the choice is clear!" As he finished the thought, he looked up to see the stately door of Simyaza's house.

He was led into the home and taken to Simyaza, who listened intently to his story. Jotham gushed with emotion as he told Simyaza of his plight. He told his tales of martyrdom within his own household and how patient he had been with his wife, hoping she would one day understand that it was all done for her. He finished by telling him how Analeah had recently even spoken poorly of Simyaza himself, "That was when I told her that I would not stand to hear any more about you. 'Simyaza has been good to us and the city of Baalta! You can speak evil of me if you want, but I will not hear it of Simyaza!' I said."

Jotham feigned an emotional shudder of his shoulders as he looked to the floor, wagging his head from side to side, "I told her that I loved her, but if she continued with that kind of talk, I would have to report her blasphemies. I can only assume that this is why she has run away. I do not know how she got past the guards at the city gates, but I have looked everywhere and cannot find her." He then clasped his hands together and looked up into Simyaza's dark eyes.

Simyaza put a boney finger to his lips and thought for a moment before speaking, "Jotham, you are a truly loyal man. I know it was not easy for you to come to me with this. Undoubtedly, you are concerned about how it will look for you in the eyes of the other men of Baalta. But, let me assure you, it is clear where your allegiances lie." He paused a moment longer before continuing, "I believe I can help you get your son back, but you know what must happen with your wife."

Jotham took a deep breath for effect, "Yes, I know. I believe, given her mindset, it would be for the best. I do not want her instilling any of her prejudices into my son. I think I have to look out for *his* best interest right now."

Simyaza smiled widely, "You are a wise man, Jotham. When we get this terrible business behind us, I think I may have a place for you. I need a man like you to handle some of Baalta's more… challenging affairs."

At this, Jotham could not hide his pleasure, "I will serve you in any way I can."

Simyaza smiled and clapped his hands as a signal to change the direction of the conversation, "Good! Now, I think I know how we can track down your wife and son." He then called to his servant, "Telah!"

The bone-thin Telah soon appeared at the door, "Yes, Master."

Simyaza spoke flatly and sternly, "Tell Jeru and Ronin to meet me out front with the wolves."

Jotham gave him a quizzical look, "Wolves?"

"Yes, wolves," Simyaza answered. "They have an amazing sense of smell. They can track a scent days after it was left. The wolves do not have to see where your wife went. They can smell where she went. Do not worry. No matter where she is, Jeru and Ronin will find her."

—◦◦◦—

Analeah had walked all day, taking a somewhat circuitous route away from Baalta. She had thought about going to her parent's farm but was afraid that would be the first place Jotham would look. In fact, she hoped that he would. Her parents' farm was in the opposite direction from the way she was headed. Perhaps it would give her that much more of a head start. The downside was that she had no idea where she was or where she was going. She stayed off the pathways as best she could and tried to hide from anyone she saw, not wanting them to be able to help her husband find her.

As the sun disappeared over the horizon, she decided to stop for the night. She had found a small lake surrounded by fig trees. There was a nearby roadway, but her sore feet could not carry her any further. Also, her aching arms could not carry her wriggling child one more moment. The lake had some large boulders between it and the roadway where she could hide.

She picked some fruit and put Asham down to play a few cubits away while she ate. Asham alternated between playing and coming by for a quick bite of the figs his mother had picked. Eventually, he tired of his play and sat in her lap. As darkness enveloped them there in the safety of the boulders, Asham drifted off to sleep. For her, sleep would not come as easily.

Chapter 6

THE HAPPY CARAVAN HAD BROKEN CAMP EARLY that morning. Enoch was the only group member who had ever been to the Royal City. In fact, he was the only one who had ever met King Seth, his grandfather's great-grandfather. For this reason, he and Ednah led the way in their oxcart, with young Mirah riding along in the bed of the cart, singing to herself and playing with her simple homemade dolls, as she often did. Following close behind were his giant friends, Gardan and his friendly behemoth, Nahla. Behind them was the large, horse-drawn carriage of Tamari's parents, Jaylon and Naamah. Riding inside the carriage were Tamari, Julis, Methuselah, and Jubal. Two of Jaylon's servants were trailing them with all the supplies needed for the journey.

Ednah leaned in close to Enoch, resting her head on his strong shoulder and linking her arm through his as he drove the oxcart along the well-worn road. She was, by nature, a woman who enjoyed the simple pleasures of the household chores of raising her children and caring for her husband. Rather than feeling trapped in a dull existence, as some of the city women would see her lot in life, Ednah thought it an honor and a blessing to see to the inner workings of the family farm.

While farm life didn't afford her many opportunities to travel about the world and see its exciting places, she was happy and content with the honest work she did at home. Though her work there was hard and sometimes rugged, she was not worn down by it. She was a strong, vibrant young woman of seventy-eight who had managed to keep the figure of her youth. Her olive skin contrasted nicely with her sandy-blonde hair, delicate features, and bright green eyes. Though a stunningly beautiful woman, she carried herself with a dignified, almost royal grace that belied her simple life.

She was, however, particularly excited about this trip. Yes, she was going to meet King Seth. But, more than that, she was going to meet the woman who gave birth to the whole of humanity, Mother Eve. She had always wanted to meet her. She wanted to look into the eyes of the first-created woman on earth. For reasons she couldn't really explain, she wanted the chance to comfort her; to embrace this woman who had been given so much yet lost even more. While, in her mind, she felt utterly unworthy of this task, her heart sang out with a yearning to ease her pain. She felt almost duty-bound to do this, so she would.

As they rode along to the rhythmic clip-clop of the oxen's hooves, Ednah took a deep breath, "We are truly blessed for this honor, are we not, Husband?"

Enoch was deep in his own thoughts, "What do you mean, Wife?"

Ednah sat up and looked at him, "I mean, to be invited to the Royal City, to be offered the Palace of King Seth *himself* in which to have our son's wedding, and to have King Seth officiate the ceremony! This is not an honor afforded to many people, is it?"

Enoch nodded in agreement, "No, my dear, it is not." He was thoughtful for a moment before speaking again, "I did not expect when I sent him notice of the wedding that he would make such an offer. When his messenger came with the invitation, he said the Lord had come to him in a dream and told him to invite us to the Royal City. I have asked the Lord about it, but He only told me to go as requested." He chuckled and shook his head in resignation, "When the King and the Creator both tell you to do something, you do it. Besides, it is a great honor, and the memory of this wedding will be one that Methuselah and Tamari cherish their whole lives."

Ednah shot a quick look into her husband's eyes, "Do you not cherish the memory of *our* wedding with just as much reverence?"

Enoch put his hand up in surrender, "Of course, I do, my sweet. Your uncle did a wonderful job officiating our ceremony. It does not matter that he had a bit too much wine and forgot my name. Nor does it matter that your father took the occasion of our wedding to introduce me to the man he had 'hoped you would marry.' Those are some of my fondest memories." He said this while overacting with a flourish of sincerity.

His feigned sincerity was not lost on Ednah as she played along and answered with a sigh while snuggling back up to him, "It *was* wonderful, wasn't it?" They both shared a deep belly laugh as Enoch kissed her on the forehead.

—◦◦◦—

From high above and behind, Gardan had been watching the two lovers closely. The giant man was always in awe of the way Enoch and his family showed their love to each other so easily. His own family situation had been so much different. The only love he had experienced had come from his mother before she was killed by his half-brother while he was helpless to stop it. Besides that, he only had his animal friends. He secretly wondered if he would ever experience the same kind of intimate, loving relationship that his small friends modeled before him.

His behemoth, Nahla, was a great friend to him. He had found her trapped in a sticky mud pit, half-starved and scared many years before. He rescued her and nursed her back to health. Since, she had not left his side and has served as his "horse," as it were. Gardan loves her immensely and is not afraid to show it, but it is not the same as the intimacy his friends shared.

Eight years before, he had another animal companion that he loved dearly. Leeno was an enormous lion who had befriended Gardan when he was feeling particularly lonely. Leeno stuck by him like the brother he wished he had, never leaving him. However, Leeno, sacrificing his own life for Gardan's, had been killed by another of Gardan's giant brothers, Skaldan.

He loved Leeno and missed him terribly, but it was still not the same. What Gardan truly longed for was the love of a family, a real family. The Creator had granted him the desires of his heart through Enoch and his family. They had opened their arms freely and loved Gardan for who he was.

To most of the world, he was a freakishly large man; the unholy spawn of a fallen angel; something to be feared, despised, and deserving of destruction. However, the Creator saw him differently. In all other cases, one such as Gardan was all those things: a mistake, unnatural, and part of the evil plot of Lucifer and his minions to taint God's creation. But the Creator took what was meant for evil and was using it for good.

While Gardan's twenty-one siblings had been born out of a hatred for mankind, he was given a different spirit altogether. The others were nourished by blood and destruction, but Gardan was given a heart that craved love and peace. He wanted no part in his father's agenda. He felt like an outcast in his own family, an alien in his own skin. He had always wondered why he was so different from his brothers.

What he couldn't know was that there was a lot more behind his birth than he was aware of.

Jaylon and Naamah drove their carriage behind Gardan, following at a safe distance so as to stay clear of the massive greenish-grey tail of Nahla as it swung, lumbering back and forth before them. In the well of the open carriage, the four young riders spoke excitedly about what the upcoming days would bring. From time to time, Jaylon or Naamah would interject something into the conversation, but they were mostly content with just listening. They would only give each other a knowing look when they heard something that could only be said out of inexperience and youth, remembering how it was when they were young and thought the same way.

As with Enoch and Ednah, Jaylon and Naamah were once simple farmers. However, it was discovered that the rocky walls of the little valley they farmed contained some of the largest and finest emeralds ever found. Their lives changed almost overnight. Suddenly, they were thrust into the upper class of their little city of Urna. They were then invited to the best parties, the most exclusive dinners, and wore the finest of clothing. Their simple farmhouse would no longer do for people of their status and was soon transformed into a palatial estate with all the amenities of the well-to-do.

However, as is often the case, their newfound wealth also brought other changes that were not for the better. They began to take on an air of self-importance. They began to treat their neighbors, who were of their own former station in life, as unimportant, less-than, underlings who they could no longer be bothered with.

This new attitude also applied to those with whom their daughters would associate. Tamari had been in love with Methuselah from a very young age, and it was all but a given that they would one day be married. But with their wealth came a new view of the simple "farm boy" in the next valley. He was no longer good enough for their daughter. They didn't want her to marry a boy of his low status, especially one whose father was so strange, one whose father actually claimed to speak to God on a regular basis.

However, despite their best efforts to separate them, the love between Tamari and Methuselah only grew stronger. Over time, and with the help of the Creator, showing His love through Methuselah's "strange" family, Jaylon and Naamah learned to shed those unhealthy attitudes toward their neighbors. In fact, over the last eight years, they had grown very close to the family of Enoch. They had developed a trust and admiration for them that they had never felt for anyone else. In light of this, they now saw Methuselah as the *only* man they would have as a son-in-law. No one else would do.

The same also applied to Methuselah's cousin, Jubal. He and Julis had been in love for about the same time as Methuselah and Tamari. Jubal shared the same depth of faith as Methuselah and treated Julis with the same love and respect. It was assumed that their marriage would not be far behind, and, as far as Jaylon and Naamah were concerned, that was just fine. They had resigned themselves to waiting for the happy arrival of the beautiful grandchildren that would result from the two unions.

They now just rode along the meandering path, Naamah nestling into her husband's shoulder, enjoying the closeness they felt with their daughters and soon-to-be sons-in-law. Naamah's heart welling with anticipation, she whispered in Jaylon's ear, "You will be a fine grandfather, Husband."

Jaylon quietly laughed, not taking his eyes off the road, "Dear Wife, you age me in the time it takes to make one statement." He paused momentarily before speaking, cognizant of how she may take to heart the same declaration about her that she had made about him. He modified it slightly, "And you shall be the most beautiful, young grandmother that ever was."

This elicited a girlish giggle, "You are truly wise, my husband. Where did you learn such wisdom?"

"Only the Lord," he responded. "Only the Lord Himself could teach someone as dense as I the wisdom necessary to please such a beguiling wife as you."

At this, they shared a giggle usually reserved for young lovers. Without realizing it, their affectionate conversation was being overheard by the youthful passengers behind them. Tamari, moved by her father's sweetness, couldn't help but respond, "Awe! That was so sweet, Father."

Surprised, Jaylon turned quickly and became a bit flush at being caught in what might be perceived by the two young men as a moment of weakness. He promptly tried to recover his manhood, clearing his throat and speaking in a deep, authoritative voice, "You know, it is not polite to listen in on other people's private conversations!" He turned his attention back to the road. Then he softened a bit before continuing, "Besides, I am just trying to show an example to Methuselah and Jubal of how I expect my daughters to be treated." He turned back, looking the two young men in the eye, "Do you two understand what I am saying?"

Methuselah and Jubal exchanged a smirk before answering in unison, "Yes, Sir." After this, the carriage was quiet but for the chuckles exchanged among the amused travelers.

Getting a little sore from the bumpy ride, Ednah asked Enoch if she could stop and stretch her legs for a while. "Of course, my dear," he answered. Then, spotting a small lake surrounded by large boulders and fruit trees, he pointed, "That looks like a good place to stop." He then motioned back to Gardan and signed his intentions. Gardan then directed Nahla to the side of the road and stopped, waiting for Jaylon to catch up, and relayed the message.

Everyone pulled to the side of the road and got out of their respective carts and carriages, stretching and yawning. Enoch and Mirah walked back toward Jaylon's carriage as Ednah, struck by the beauty of the scene before her, took several steps toward the lake. She scanned the area and took notice of the stately fig trees encompassing the lake. The mid-morning sun perfectly reflected the landscape, and the many colorful birds sang out their songs among the branches and boulders upon which they were perched.

Looking back to her left, some movement caught her eye from behind one of the boulders. She took a second look but saw nothing for a moment and took another step in that direction. That was when she noticed a pair of bright blue eyes peering at her from behind the massive rock. When those eyes saw that she had spotted them, they disappeared with a giggle.

Ednah thought, "What would a young child be doing out here alone?" She decided to investigate. As she rounded the boulder, she saw a young boy standing beside his sleeping mother. One look at her and Ednah could tell that the young mother was exhausted. She had to be not to notice the noisy caravan pulling up only cubits away.

She started to approach but thought better of it and gave a gentle smile to the boy before turning back to inform Enoch of her find. As she rounded the boulder, she was met by Enoch, who spoke loudly, "There you are!"

Ednah quickly touched his lips to quiet him as she whispered, "Shhh."

Enoch was a bit surprised and taken aback, "What is it? Why do I have to whisper? Are you afraid I'm going to wake someone up?" He said this with a smirk because the idea of anyone sleeping in this remote place was absurd.

He got his answer, "Yes. There is a woman sleeping against one of the boulders over there. She has a very young boy with her. The poor girl looks to be exhausted and I don't want to startle her."

Enoch gave her a quizzical look and inched his way around the corner to see for himself. He then slowly came back to Ednah. He thought for a moment before speaking, "Go tell the others to try and be quiet. I cannot imagine why she would be out here with such a small child like this. Keep everyone where they are for now. I need to pray about this. Perhaps she needs our help."

Ednah walked back toward the road as Enoch returned to the lake and began praying. However, it was not long before he heard footsteps behind him again. Turning, he said, "I thought I told you…" Then, he realized that it was not Ednah who had approached him as he dropped to one knee, "Lord, forgive me! I did not know…"

The Lord smiled at him and stopped him short, "You *were* speaking to me, were you not?"

The Lord motioned for Enoch to get up as he fumbled for an answer, "Yes, Lord. I was speaking to you, but I do not always know when you are going to appear like this. It is always a surprise to me."

The Creator chuckled a bit at Enoch's answer, "This is why I appear to you this way, Enoch. It is because you always tell me exactly the truth. In you there is no guile."

Enoch bowed his head reverently, "Thank you, Lord. You are kind to speak well of me. I am truly blessed."

The Lord changed the subject to the matter at hand, "This young woman and her child are the very reason I have brought you out here today. It is true that I wanted to bless you and Ednah with a memorable wedding for your son. However, I also have an important task for you. This woman has been through a terrible ordeal. I want you to take her with you to the Royal City. Her story needs to be heard by King Seth. I also want you and Methuselah to help him rectify the situation she will tell him about. It will not be a pleasant task for any of you, but I will be with you. No matter what, do not despair. When it looks as if all hope may be lost and you are at your weakest, I will be there to show My strength."

Enoch bowed his head again, "Yes, Lord. I will do as you say." When he looked back up, the Creator was gone. Enoch then walked back to his now-curious fellow travelers to relay the message. After some debate, it was decided that a woman's touch was needed here.

Chapter 7

ANALEAH'S NIGHT HAD BEEN A RESTLESS ONE. IT HAD taken her a long time to settle her thoughts enough to fall asleep. Although she had her son, she couldn't help feeling alone in this new place, both in terms of the wilderness and her life. Her mind had raced with the anxiety of her unique situation, "Where does this journey end? What will be my destination? How will I explain my lack of a husband to people? Should I lie and tell them he is dead? As far as I am concerned, he *is* dead…to me, anyway. Or should I just find a place of solitude where Asham and I can make a life for ourselves? What do I do? Who can I trust? Oh, God! Help me!"

This set of questions kept replaying in her mind. The sequence would change, but the terror of the unknown always brought her back to her final plea, "Oh, God! Help me!" She wasn't sure when, but the gift of sleep finally, mercifully, came to her.

It seemed as if she had only closed her eyes for a moment when the hard boulder she leaned against started becoming unbearable, nudging her back to consciousness. Her eyelids were heavy and unmovable. She could sense daylight beyond them but wanted no part of it. However, she could also feel Asham stirring around next to her. No matter how tired she was, her duties as a mother came before her own comfort.

She took a deep breath and stretched, licking her dry lips. "Good morning, Little One," she said groggily as she stretched a little more raising her arms to the sky. She finally pushed her eyes open. She instantly blinked and recoiled at what she saw, eyes fully open now.

"Do not be afraid," Ednah said this as softly and tenderly as she could, holding out her hands, open-palmed, and standing back a bit. She remained quiet as she watched the terrified woman bolt up from her resting place and scramble to get hold of her son protectively. This time Naamah decided to try and soothe her, "We are sorry to have startled you. We mean you no harm."

Analeah quickly turned her head from side to side to get her bearings on the situation, scanning her surroundings to see if more people were around besides these two women. Seeing no one else, she tried stepping back to distance herself from her intruders, only to find that the boulder she had slept against blocked her path. She shrieked a panicked question, "Who are you?!" Before allowing an answer, she asked another in the same shrill voice, "What do you want?!"

Ednah replied with an understanding smile and a quiet voice, "I am Ednah, and this is Naamah. We mean you no harm. We do not want anything. We were only concerned for you and your son." Naamah nodded in agreement and smiled reassuringly, her hands folded over her heart.

Analeah stood silently for a while, digesting the information. Her whirling mind began to slow, and her panic began to subside slightly. She could now see that the two women didn't seem to be a threat, but she was still a bit wary. She sternly responded calmly but resolutely, "My son and I want to be left alone! I appreciate your concern, but we are fine. We were only resting here."

Ednah again smiled at her and held up her hands in surrender, "Alright. Again, we are sorry to have startled you. We only wanted to see if there was anything we could do for you."

Naamah could still see the fear in the woman's eyes. Her heart went out to her, and she wanted to try and put her at ease if she could, "We were just on our way to the Royal City for our daughter's wedding." She then pointed toward Ednah, "She is going to marry her son. We only just stopped here for a rest. Then, Ednah saw your son playing amongst the boulders."

Analeah thought about what Naamah had said before replying, "The Royal City?" She had heard of it but had no idea where it was. "Is that where this road leads?"

Ednah then realized the young woman didn't even know where she was. She decided not to call attention to her troubling question but only answer it innocently, "Yes, I think so. I have never been there myself, but my husband has. He is the one who is leading our caravan."

Analeah's heart jumped, "There are more of you?"

Naamah could see that this seemed to upset her, "It is only our two families and some friends. I assure you, no one means you any harm." She paused momentarily before asking, "Would you like something to eat or drink? You look exhausted. We have plenty." Ednah smiled and nodded in agreement.

Analeah thought for a moment. She didn't want to risk being discovered by anyone loyal to Simyaza. But none of Simyaza's followers were ever as nice as these people seemed to be. She also knew that, besides whatever fruit she could find along the way, she had nothing else to feed her son. She was also getting very hungry. She decided to accept the offer, "If it is not too much trouble, we would like something to eat."

Genuinely delighted, Ednah smiled and reached out her hand, "What is your name?"

Analeah approached her but decided not to take her hand and kept some distance between them. She also decided it might be better not to use her real name with these strangers. The less they knew, the better. She scrambled for a name and came up with her mother's, "My name is Naomi. My son's name is Joaz."

It hurt as soon as it left her lips. She momentarily wrestled with herself, "Why did I use *that* name? I should change it! I should have never given them that name!" She fought back the tears as she followed behind the women, "It is too late now. If I try to change his name now, it will look suspicious." She prayed silently that these people would not say it too much, sparing her the emotional death that her firstborn's name brought every time she heard it said aloud.

Ednah led the way around the enormous boulders toward the rest of the caravan. When she turned the last corner and saw them, a thought came to mind, and she turned and held up a hand, stopping her followers short, "Naomi, have you ever seen a giant?"

Analeah was caught entirely off guard by the question, "A giant? What do you mean?"

Ednah struggled momentarily with an answer, "Well, one of our friends is a giant. His name is Gardan. I did not want you to be startled again when you saw him. I assure you, he is as gentle as a dove, but his appearance may be… a bit shocking to you."

Analeah looked over at Naamah, who nodded in agreement, then back to Ednah, "When you say 'giant,' do you mean he is just very large?"

Ednah nodded with emphasis, "Yes. Very, *very* large." Naamah again signaled her agreement.

Analeah gave a quizzical look, "I have heard that there are giant men, but I thought that those were just stories. Do you mean they actually exist?"

Naamah decided to answer this time, "Yes, they actually exist. However, as Ednah said, Gardan is as gentle as a dove. He is a dear friend who would never hurt anyone unprovoked. Ednah just didn't want you to be frightened when you saw him."

Analeah was wary but curious, "Alright."

Ednah smiled and nodded. She then turned and continued around the corner. When the caravan came into view, she stopped and stepped aside, waiting to see her guest's reaction.

Analeah held Asham tightly, not sure what to expect. When she rounded the corner and the rest of the strangers came into view, she could not hold back a gasp when she saw Gardan. Even Asham jumped a bit at the sight of the giant man who was three times taller than the other men in the group, "Oooooh!" said Asham as he pointed his little finger at Gardan.

Enoch, realizing what had stopped their guests in their tracks, stepped forward and introduced himself, "Good morning! I am Enoch, Ednah's husband. We are glad to meet you."

Analeah didn't take her eyes off of Gardan. She was stunned by the sheer size of the man. The fact that he stood next to a behemoth had not even registered to her yet. She finally glanced for a moment at Enoch before returning her gaze toward Gardan again. "He is huge," was all she could manage to mumble.

Gardan could see her shock and began to feel a bit uncomfortable. Methuselah could see Gardan's discomfort and decided to try and make him feel better, "Do not worry, Gardan. She has just never seen anyone as handsome as you before."

This elicited a smile from Gardan, "Perhaps you are right, my friend."

Ednah jumped in to break up the awkwardness of the moment. She put her hand on her guest's back, "I would like to introduce everyone to Naomi and her son, Joaz."

The mention of that name snapped Analeah out of her stare. She didn't say anything. She only nodded.

Ednah continued, "Naomi, you have already met my husband, Enoch." She led her around the group one by one. "This is Naamah's husband, Jaylon. This is our son, Methuselah, and his cousin, Jubal. These two beautiful girls are my soon-to-be daughter-in-law, Tamari, and her sister, Julis. This is our daughter, Mirah. And…" Ednah gently led her toward Gardan, who decided to make himself a little less scary to the obviously shocked woman and her child by kneeling. Ednah continued, "This is our dear friend, Gardan."

Analeah slowly nodded, "Hello."

Gardan smiled his most disarming smile, "Hello, Naomi. Hello, Little One."

Analeah was glad that he chose not to say his name. She was also struck by how gentle he was and that he had a very nice smile. She thought she would explain herself, "I am sorry for staring at you that way. I have just never seen anyone as big as you before and…"

Gardan raised a hand and stopped her, "There is no need. If I were in your place, I might be just as shocked. In fact, the first time I saw one of you little people, I was a bit out of sorts myself." He gave a little chuckle, along with the rest of the group.

Analeah was suddenly and completely at ease with the massive man. There was something about him that she liked instantly, "You are very kind." She then turned her attention to the behemoth behind him, "And who is this?"

Gardan was now the one staring and had to snap himself back to the conversation, "Oh. This is Nahla. A better and more faithful friend, you will not find."

Analeah was impressed by her sheer size and apparent tameness, "I have seen them from afar, but have never been so close to one before. Can I touch her?"

Gardan laughed again, "Nahla would be offended if you didn't!" He turned to Nahla and called her, "Nahla, come say hello to our new friends." Nahla then brought her long neck around and gently sniffed Analeah and Asham, allowing them to rub her nose while she made a deep purring sound from her belly. Asham laughed and squealed his approval.

As the group watched the proceedings, Naamah leaned over and whispered to Ednah, "Did you see what I saw a moment ago?"

Ednah looked at her with a raised eyebrow, "You saw it too? I thought it was just me."

After a while, the group ate their lunch and started preparing to continue on their way. Once she felt her new friend was at ease, Ednah decided to make an invitation to her, "Naomi, if you don't mind me asking, where are you and your son heading?"

Analeah thought for a moment. She did not want to get anyone else involved in her problems, but she felt as though she could trust these people. Besides, she really didn't know where she was going. These people were going to the Royal City, and she didn't want to spend another night alone, "I am also going to the Royal City."

Knowing that Naomi was not being entirely truthful, Ednah smiled widely, "Well, since that is where we are going, would you like to come along with us? We have plenty of room."

Analeah was grateful for the offer, "If you are sure, and it will not be too much trouble?"

Naamah responded from behind, "No trouble at all. In fact, if Ednah had not asked you, I would have."

The caravan was soon on its way.

Chapter 8

*J*OTHAM HAD FOLLOWED JERU AND RONIN ALL NIGHT. The search party had not stopped for anything. It was all Jotham could do to keep up with Simyaza's huntsmen. It was all the two huntsmen could do to keep up with the two massive wolves that practically dragged them along the unseen scent trail of their prey.

When they began their search, Jotham had supplied them with a piece of Analeah's clothing. They met up at the main gate to the city, but the wolves had only sniffed around in circles with nothing to show for their trouble. After some time, Jeru suggested they begin again from Jotham's house. After a few fits and starts, they managed to discern between her regular travels within the city and her escape route.

Several scent trails led toward the city square or the bakery. However, when one of them seemed to lead toward the city's furnace, Jotham instantly knew she wouldn't have gone that way. She would not even look that way unless she had to. "She used the livestock gate to escape," Jotham said.

With a smirk, Ronin responded in his gravelly voice, "She is a cunning woman." Jeru agreed. The other scents of that part of the city were overpowering and made it difficult for the wolves to pick up the lesser scent of Analeah. They finally decided to exit the city and get a reasonable distance away before resuming their search.

Jeru made an inquiry of Jotham. "In the interest of time, do you have any idea as to which direction she was likely to go? Does she have some friends or family nearby?"

Jotham thought about it and pointed south, "Her parents have a farm that way. She would probably go there."

Jeru and Ronin nodded to each other as they took turns rubbing Analeah's clothing into the wolves' noses again to re-establish the target scent. They made a wide circular swath toward the south until they had reached the banks of a river, which a woman and a child would not have been able to cross. Ronin and Jeru exchanged another smirk. Ronin turned back to Jotham, "As I said before, she is a cunning woman. If she had gone this way, the wolves would have picked up her trail by now. She expected that you would go to her family's farm first. She bought herself more time by going a different direction." He pointed back toward the north. "We will circle back this way. We will find her trail unless she grew wings and *flew* away from the city." Jotham and Jeru nodded their agreement.

The sun had begun to appear by the time they found her trail. She had not made it easy for them. There were roads and pathways throughout the area. Still, her scent trail would only cross over them and rarely follow one of them for very long before changing directions again. Jeru and Ronin grew increasingly impressed with her as they went along. Occasionally, they would just look at each other and shake their heads. Other times, one would comment, "Smart woman."

Jotham was beginning to tire of their growing admiration for the woman who had stolen his son. He finally barked at them, "Listen to me! That woman has taken my son from me! As far as I am concerned, she is *not* 'smart' or 'cunning,' as you two keep suggesting! She is nothing more than a thief!

I would appreciate it if you kept your comments to yourself and found her! She must *pay* for what she has done to me. Do you understand?"

Jeru and Ronin gave each other a perturbed look before Ronin walked over and got uncomfortably close to Jotham. He spoke slowly and clearly in a guttural growl, "You listen to *me*. Obviously, this woman is smarter and more cunning than you because *none* of your suggestions have helped in this effort at all. In fact, if it was not for the wolves, I do not believe you would *ever* find your wife and son." Ronin began to turn away before he had another thought, "You know, Jotham, I am actually beginning to see why she left in the first place. Do *you* understand *me*?!"

Jotham's anger was rising in his throat, "Now you..." It was then that the wolf on Ronin's chain bared his teeth at him and growled menacingly. Jotham decided not to continue his thought. The three men remained silent for the rest of the morning as they continued.

Jotham could not help but notice the sudden changes in landscapes as they took their circuitous route through the lands that led away from Baalta. One farm would be lush and green, full of life. Yet, another farm would be dry and desolate, devoid of even grass. Simyaza had said that he would "bless" the lands of those who followed him. He also said that he would "curse" the lands of those who refused.

It was quite evident to Jotham whose land was whose. In fact, he had seen his own fields starting to wither away until he had made his "sacrifice" to Simyaza. Now, his farm produced more than ever before, increasing his wealth and stature in the community. Simyaza's power was undeniable.

However, as they traveled further away from Baalta, he also could not help but notice that all the farmlands outside of the immediate area around Baalta were flourishing. A thought came to mind, "Perhaps Simyaza's power has limits." He quickly brushed those blasphemous ideas away, "Simyaza has kept all his promises. He has been a man of his word and done everything he said he would. He is truly worthy of our praises and adoration." He tried not to think about it anymore after that, keeping his thoughts on the matter at hand.

The sun had passed its apex by the time they came upon a small lake surrounded by large fig trees and boulders. The wolves quickly zeroed in on the spot where Analeah had slept. The grass was still a bit matted down, and Asham's small footprints were easily seen in the sand near the lake's edge.

Jeru made his observations clear, "She slept here." He bent down and picked up more evidence of his findings, "Here are the husks of some of the figs she was eating. These were eaten last night. They are beginning to dry out a little."

Ronin then assessed the situation further, "She was already here by the time we began our search early this morning but, carrying a young child, she must have been exhausted. She probably woke up late. We haven't stopped all night. Therefore, we have made up quite a bit of ground on her. It shouldn't be long now before we catch up to her."

Jeru had been investigating further in the meantime and had made more discoveries of his own as he followed her scent around the boulders out to the road. He hollered out to Ronin and Jotham, who quickly made their way to where he was, "She seems to have made some friends here. You can see many more foot…" Something stopped him cold. He motioned for Ronin to come over to the spot he was standing and pointed down to the road. Ronin immediately saw what had gotten his attention. The two men looked at each other and then back to the ground as one of them placed a foot next to one of the footprints.

Jotham came up to see what was of so much interest, "What is it?" Then he saw a footprint three times the size of the man's foot. After a shake of his head, he tried to make sense of what he was seeing, "Is that a…man's footprint?"

Jeru was the first to speak, "Simyaza told me that there were giant men on this earth, and I have heard stories, but I have never seen one for myself." He paused to ponder it, "I thought they were just unusually large men, but the man who made this is more than large. Judging from the size of his foot, he must be twelve or fifteen cubits tall!"

All three men were quiet for a time as they all took turns looking around to find something that big to try and picture in their minds. After investigating further, Jeru made a few new discoveries that he shared with the others, "Do you want to hear something even stranger? You can see several tracks made by oxcarts. Look, you can see that they all stopped here for a time. But, it also appears that there was a behemoth traveling with them. Does that make any sense to you?"

Ronin began to shake his head when something he had heard a few years back came to mind, "Wait. I remember hearing something a few years ago. It was before Simyaza first came to Baalta. I heard that there was a giant living near a small city to the east called Urna. Have you heard Simyaza go on his rants about the man named Enoch, who claims to speak with God?" The men nodded their recognition before Ronin continued, "Well, I heard that this giant was a friend of Enoch, and that he had a pet behemoth that he would ride as if it were a horse."

Jeru and Jotham gave him a look of disbelief, raising their eyebrows at such a preposterous statement. Ronin recognized their looks of disbelief, "Well, do either of you have a better explanation for what we are seeing here?"

Jeru had to admit, "No. I suppose I do not."

Jotham interjected, "If that is so, then what does that mean?"

Ronin thought for a moment before answering, "Perhaps nothing. It is possible that Analeah had already gone when the giant and his friends stopped here. We will see where the scent leads us." The two huntsmen spurred on their wolves to track the scent again. The wolves went back to the lakeside and then back to the road, then back to the lakeside. It was becoming apparent what had happened.

"It appears as though our prey was picked up by this... mysterious caravan," Jeru said. "Their tracks should be easy enough to follow, but what will we do when we find them? If she is being protected by the giant and this man, Enoch, the job is going to become a lot more...complicated than a simple retrieval."

Jotham's anger began to flare again, "I do not care who is protecting her! I want my son back! He is *my* son and I have a right to have him back!"

Jeru gave him a menacing look, "You need to watch your temper when you speak to us! We work for Simyaza, *not* for you! He gave us a job and we will do it. But, the situation has just changed. It now appears that this man, Enoch, is involved, and I believe that is something that Simyaza would want to know about." Jeru rubbed his chin for a moment before continuing. He looked over at the two men and the wolves as he formulated a plan of action, "Ronin, you and Jotham should take one of the wolves back to Baalta. I will follow these tracks and see where they lead. I will keep the woman's clothing so that, if she left the caravan, I can continue tracking her. If not, then I can see what the situation is and devise a plan from there."

Jotham bristled at the idea, "I am not going back to Baalta without my..."

"You will do as I say!" snapped Jeru. "We will get your son. But it will be on *Simyaza's* terms, or mine. *You* will just have to be patient. Do we understand each other?" Jotham only responded with a huff. "Now, you go tell Simyaza what the situation is and I will meet you back here in two days. That will give me enough time to assess the circumstances and I will inform you of what I have found."

Without a word, Ronin nodded and walked briskly toward Baalta. Jotham tried again, "But…"

Ronin never turned around. He only barked his orders, "Let's go!" Jotham followed reluctantly.

Chapter 9

BEFORE LEAVING THE PLACE WHERE THEY HAD found their new companions, Enoch made a thoughtful suggestion to Ednah, "Perhaps it would be better for Naomi and Joaz if they rode with you and Naamah in the back of our oxcart so she will feel more at ease."

Ednah liked that suggestion, "That is a good idea. We can put down some soft blankets to make it more comfortable."

Mirah, who had been listening to their private conversation, as she was often known to do, was dying for the chance to play with a real baby instead of her doll. She jumped right in with her own suggestion. "I can ride along too and take care of Joaz!" she said excitedly. "That way, Naomi can rest. She looks like she could really use some rest." She slightly overacted on this last statement, but her logic was sound.

After exchanging a glance at each other, Enoch and Ednah agreed. Ednah turned to find some soft blankets, and Mirah giggled slightly as she followed her. Enoch gently caught Mirah's arm before she got away and whispered in her ear, "We have talked before about your listening to other people's private conversations, haven't we, Little One?" Mirah, a bit embarrassed and ashamed, nodded. Feeling that his statement had done its job, Enoch softened his gaze and kissed her on the head. "Go ahead and help your mother." She smiled at him and skipped away. Enoch gave a little laugh and shook his head before going to tell the others of the new plan.

The women tried to talk with their new companion and get to know her a little better along the way. Still, Ednah and Naamah found it difficult to get any answers of substance from her. She would only answer with a "yes" or "no." Other times, she would only give an even more cryptic shrug of the shoulders and look away without another word. The only information they were getting was being spoken in volumes without a word; "This woman has been hurt; she is scared to death and in a lot of pain!"

They had been riding for quite a while now, and the scenery was starting to look a bit different. Enoch could see that they were getting nearer to the Royal City. Open fields were giving way to small farms as they steadily rode uphill. From time to time, between trees, the surprisingly small but regal Royal City would come into view where it sat perched atop the low mountain.

They were passing a tiny, exquisitely flowered farmhouse when Enoch noticed a very dirty man working in the black soil of one of the gardens near the house. Watching the man work was a small, frail-looking woman leaning on a wooden rake. After a double-take at the man, Enoch suddenly pulled up on the reins to stop the cart. This brought some inquisitive looks from his riders, who turned to see what had caught his attention.

"Oh, look at the beautiful flowers!" said Naamah, who didn't even notice the filthy man standing in the garden. The rest of the women followed in kind, all except for Analeah. She reacted with more fear than awe and quickly turned her head back around and busied herself by straightening her clothing and pulling her hair down on one side to cover her face a bit. Her reaction was not lost on Ednah, but she filed it away in her mind and looked back to the scene before her.

When the gardener looked up and saw Enoch, he smiled widely and started toward them. The mischievous gardener could see that Enoch was about to speak and quickly spoke over him to keep him quiet, "Hello, strangers!" The last word came with a purposeful look at Enoch, who smiled wryly at the man. "I know just about everyone around here, but I do not recall ever seeing you lovely people before."

Naamah spoke up, "Your garden is beautiful! I have never seen such an array of exquisite flowers in one place before."

The gardener turned and scanned the garden quickly before turning back to the onlookers, "That is very kind of you to say, but I cannot take any credit for it. The Creator made them beautiful and", pointing back toward the kind-looking woman in the garden with a flourish of his hand, "Tara here directed their planting. I am but a humble worker who has the honor of placing them where I am told." The woman's face turned a bit flush, and she waived him off with a shake of her head and a chuckle.

The man turned back to the onlookers with a broad smile that made him easily likable, "I take it you are all headed to the Royal City?"

Enoch had to fight a chuckle of his own, "Yes. We are going to see King Seth. He is going to perform the wedding for our son, Methuselah."

The man smiled even wider and clapped his dirty hands together, "That is wonderful! I *love* weddings!" He then looked expectantly at Enoch. "If it would not be imposing on you, do you think I could attend?"

Enoch turned back to Ednah with a questioning glance. Ednah was taken aback by the stranger's forwardness but nodded her nervous approval. Almost as an afterthought, she added a stipulation, "We would be glad to have you if it is alright with King Seth."

Enoch turned back to the stranger with a reserved look, "Yes, I suppose my wife is right. That decision would be up to the king. Do you know him?"

The stranger laughed heartily, "Oh, the king and I have known each other for as long as I can remember! As a matter of fact, I believe I have attended every wedding he has ever performed." He turned his attention to the women in the cart, "Please, introduce me to the lovely ladies you have with you."

Enoch gladly did so, naming his riders one by one, to which the gardener replied to each, "Truly, a pleasure!" When introduced to Joaz, he tickled the little one's belly and laughed along with his reaction. He then turned to his mother and spoke kindly, "This is a lovely little man you have here. God has truly blessed you." Upon saying this, he could not help but notice that his comment seemed to elicit a look of pain on the face of the woman. This puzzled him a bit, but he graciously didn't show it.

At this, he clapped his hands together again and turned his attention back to the rest of the caravan. Upon approaching Gardan and Nahla, he whistled in awe. The man was impressed by the sheer size of the two of them together, "You must be Gardan."

Gardan was a little surprised at this, "How do you know who I am, Sir?"

The man chuckled, "My giant friend, everyone in the Royal City, and I dare say, the entire earth has heard of you and your beautiful companion here." With this, he bowed deeply and caressed the underside of Nahla's neck as she gently sniffed him.

He now walked back to the carriage of Jaylon and the four riders who, by this time, had dismounted and were stretching from the long ride. Once again, he smiled widely, approaching them, "Who do I have the pleasure of meeting now?"

Jaylon did not know quite what to make of this dirty man. As a city leader in Urna, he was used to being treated with a certain amount of reverence when being addressed by people of what he considered to be the lower classes of life. However, the man was amiable and seemed to mean no harm, so Jaylon introduced himself. He was surprised when the man gave him a look of recognition.

The gardener's eyes widened, "Are you the same Jaylon that has the emerald mines?"

Jaylon now felt he was getting a little more of the respect he deserved, "I am he." He was slightly surprised again when the man suddenly turned his attention away from him and toward the others.

The gardener took one look at Methuselah and turned back to Enoch, "This must be the son that is being married! He has your features." Enoch only nodded in the affirmative. The man turned back to Methuselah and slapped him on the back, "Congratulations, young man! Now, tell me which of these lovely creatures is to be your wife."

Methuselah proudly put his hand on his bride-to-be's shoulder, "This is Tamari."

The man only smiled and said one word, "Beautiful!"

Methuselah waited for Jaylon to introduce the others but could see that he was less than amused by the proceedings and decided to take over, "This is my cousin, Jubal, and this is Jaylon's other daughter, Julis."

The man bowed graciously at each introduction, then, to Jaylon's shock, turned back to the last cart and his two servants. He spoke to them in the same respectful way that he had spoken with everyone else; that is, everyone but Jaylon himself, as he saw it. Everyone in the caravan, including his servants, liked this man very much. But Jaylon did not.

After a rather lengthy conversation with the servants, the man made his way back to the cart of Enoch. He turned to the woman standing in the garden and asked pleadingly, "Tara, dear, do you think we could finish our work another day? I need to attend to some things in the city." The woman smiled and nodded. He waved to her and turned to Enoch, "Do you think I could ride into the city with you?"

"Of course," said Enoch. "We would be happy to have you ride along."

The rest of the way into the city, Ednah studied the man intently. There seemed to be something about this dirty man that she recognized, but she could not figure out what it was. He was tall with muscular features. The latter, she decided, was due to his gardening work. From his greying hair, she could see that he was not a very young man, but he had an almost childlike way about him. He had very bright green eyes and an infectious smile that seemed to make everyone else smile with him. And his skin seemed to be dark, but he was also filthy, so it was hard to tell.

All the physical features were easy to see. However, it was something else that she could not seem to place. He carried himself in a rather strange way for a servant. She thought that perhaps it was just his jovial personality that was throwing her. This, she finally figured, was just the way people in this area acted because, as they went along, everyone they passed seemed to be the friendliest people she had ever seen. No matter what the people were doing, they would drop everything to waive and welcome them. The gardener would waive to them, and the people seemed so anxious to reciprocate in kind. She thought it strange, but very nice also.

As they approached the main gate leading into the city, the gardener asked if he could get out of the cart before entering. Enoch obliged him. The man thanked Enoch for his hospitality and waited as the caravan passed, waiving as they passed. Ednah turned to Enoch, "You know, he never even told us his name."

Enoch replied simply, "I am sure we will see him again."

Chapter 10

U NLIKE URNA, THE ROYAL CITY HAD WIDE OPEN
lanes that could easily be navigated toward the city's
center where the King lived. Even Gardan and Nahla found
it roomy enough. However, Gardan kept an eye on her colossal tail, which she habitually swung widely as she walked.
The people of the city were used to having all kinds of visitors. However, the sight of the two giants going through town
brought out many onlookers, making it appear as if they were
part of a parade of sorts. They finally entered the courtyard
in front of the king's residence. They gathered together, dis-
mounting their respective carriages as they gazed around at
their surroundings.

The courtyard was laid out in a giant square and decorated
with exquisitely designed flowerboxes set in mathematically
precise intervals around the outer edges. The entire square was
paved with huge, almost polished, flat stones of all colors—
grey, red, beige, yellow, blue, and pink. These, too, were laid
out with mathematical precision so that no stones of like color
were touching. Each color stone was equidistant from the next
stone of that same color.

The King's residence was also built from the same stones,
although they were cut much smaller than the paving stones.
The same precision was given to them as the courtyard, the

only difference being that the stones used to build the residence were not as polished. This had the effect of giving a person a feeling of awe yet also making them feel welcome. There was no mistake that you were entering a palace, yet there were also enough rough edges that you thought you were entering a home.

As the group stood admiring the scene, the large doors leading from the residence to the center of the courtyard opened wide. A well-dressed servant peered out and smiled at the visitors, turned back into the home, then came back out with another servant dressed the same way, and they held the doors open. Then, a man and woman came out with broad, welcoming smiles of their own.

Enoch recognized them immediately and turned to Ednah, "Dear, I know how long you have wanted this! Are you ready?" Ednah gave him an excited look and straightened her clothes to make herself more presentable as she turned to meet the two greeters.

The man was as handsome a man as she had ever seen. His hair was almost white with touches of grey throughout. Still, his bright blue eyes drew all your attention immediately away from any signs of age. He was not overly muscular but cut a fine figure. His tunic was simple, but he wore it with royal dignity.

The woman was, for lack of a better word, stunning. Her hair was a bit darker than that of her husband. However, her dark, olive-toned skin was without blemish. Her eyes were large, a blue-green color that Ednah had never before seen. She wore a wrap-around style of dress striped in a light blue and white that seemed to make her hair look darker than it was. What struck Ednah most was that a woman of over seven hundred years still managed to keep the shapely figure of a woman one-seventh her age. She was awestruck at the sight of her.

Enoch made the long-awaited introductions as they approached: "Father Adam, Mother Eve, I would like you to meet my wife, Ednah."

Adam spoke first. "Hello, Daughter. I have asked this husband of yours to bring you to meet us several times before, but he is always full of excuses. I now see why. He was afraid we would ask him how he talked such a pretty young woman into marrying him." He chuckled deeply at his little joke. Ednah was so nervous that she only smiled as her face flushed at the compliment.

Eve lightly scolded her husband, "Adam!" She then turned back to Ednah and leaned in with a gentle hug and kiss on the cheek, "Ednah, it is wonderful to finally meet you. How was your journey?"

Ednah finally found her tongue, "I have wanted to meet you for such a long time! I have so many things I would like to ask you! I can't believe I finally get to meet you!" She suddenly realized she hadn't even taken a breath between sentences and took one now. "I am sorry to gush at you like that. It's just that I have been so anxious to meet you."

Eve smiled graciously at her and hugged her again, "That is quite alright, Daughter. I believe I have been just as anxious to meet you." She looked around at the others, nervously awaiting their turns, and put her arm around her, "Now, please introduce me to the rest of my family."

Enoch and Ednah took the revered couple around and made the presentations to everyone in the party. Eve took a particular interest in the women. After Ednah had finished with the family members, she searched for Naomi and Joaz but could not immediately find them until she noticed Naomi trying to hide behind the horses that had been pulling Jaylon's carriage.

She turned to Eve and whispered, "Mother Eve, we found a young mother and child along the road during our journey.

However, I am not quite sure what to make of them. We have tried to find out more about her, but her answers have been very evasive. She seems to be a sweet girl, but it is obvious that she is very frightened about something. In fact, she is hiding behind those horses right now. I feel she needs some help. What do you think we should do?"

Eve thought for a moment, "Let me see if I can get her to talk to me." With that, she nonchalantly made her way to where the woman was hiding.

When Analeah saw her approaching, her heart nearly jumped out of her chest, but it was too late to try and hide again. She took a deep breath and turned to face her but couldn't bring herself to look into Eve's eyes. She only spoke timidly, "Hello."

"Hello, Daughter," was all that Eve said. She decided to let that hang in the air for a few moments.

Analeah was struck. It was only two words, but they were spoken directly to her by the mother of humanity. The word "Daughter" stabbed at her heart. Her mind raced. She thought of her own mother. She longed for the comfort she would feel from a heart-to-heart conversation with her mother right now! Tears were coming! She wanted to stop them, but it was too late. They were already streaming down her face. She had tried not to feel anything for so long, but she now thought she would burst. She looked up for a quick glance into this woman's eyes to see what she expected to be a bewildered look. However, when she did, she saw compassion behind big, blue-green eyes that were moist with their own tears.

Eve could feel the poor girl's pain deep within herself. She didn't know why there was such pain, but that didn't matter. There was pain, and that was enough for her. She then did what came naturally for any mother; she reached out to hold and comfort one of her hurting children.

That was all it took. Analeah was undone. Her body heaved as her sobs were emptied into the bosom of this kind mother of all humanity; for this moment at least, *her* mother.

—◦◦◦—

Adam took particular interest in the men of the party, especially Gardan. He had never seen a giant before and was enthralled by the massive man. He spoke to him at length, asking question after question, all the while stroking Nahla's neck as she nuzzled up to him, purring deeply. Adam liked Gardan very much and found him to be genuine and sincere. The feeling was mutual as Gardan got down on one knee to show respect to the great man and to speak to him eye to eye.

The other men had gathered around and listened intently to their conversation when the women approached; all the women except Eve and Naomi. Enoch looked over at Ednah, who knew his question before he asked it. She only pointed to where the two women were sobbing in each other's arms. Enoch saw what she was pointing out and smiled back at her, gently touching her back. He whispered to her, "That was why we were to come here."

She whispered back to him, "We also came to see our son married by King Seth." They exchanged another smile. She then had another thought, "When do we meet him anyway?"

Enoch smiled at her, "Sooner than you think."

She gave him an inquisitive look but didn't have a chance to ask anything else before Adam spoke up, "Well, I suppose you weary travelers would probably like something to eat and to get a rest after your long trip. It will get dark soon, and we should get you settled into your rooms." Almost as an afterthought, he turned back to Gardan, "Gardan, my large friend, I am sorry that the house is not quite big enough to accommodate you. I will have to see about erecting a tent for you outside. Would that be alright?"

Gardan replied politely, "Do not go to any trouble for me and Nahla. We will be fine in the open air. We do not really like to be too confined anyway."

Adam nodded in agreement, "I understand. The rest of you, follow me. We will have your horses and oxen cared for. Just get what you need out of your carriages and bring them in with you."

Jaylon turned to his servants and gave his own orders, "You two men stay with the carriage and horses. I will find a place for you to stay tonight."

Adam stopped in his tracks and turned on his heels. He looked directly into Jaylon's eyes, "Jaylon, your men will stay in the house with the rest of us. We have plenty of room. They are my children as much as any of you are." Without another word, he turned back around and led the group into the house.

Jaylon did not know what to say. He was a guest here and could not argue with his host. However, his pride, wounded twice in one day, ached. He thought, "I cannot wait until I return to Urna, where I will get the proper respect that I deserve!"

On the way toward the house, Ednah and Naamah made their way over to Eve and Naomi. Eve saw them coming and continued to hold onto the crying woman. She quietly waived them on into the house, signaling they would be in soon.

—⁓—

Jeru had followed the road for some time, carefully watching for any signs that his quarry had left the path. Occasionally, he would rub the piece of clothing with Analeah's scent into the wolf's nose. He finally came to a place where it appeared as though the caravan had stopped. There, he saw the little cottage surrounded by flower gardens. Even *he* was struck by the beauty that lay before him. He allowed himself a moment to drink in the sight.

Then, he noticed a small, frail-looking woman tending the soil. "Hello!" he hollered to the woman. She looked up at him, nodded silently, and returned to her work. "I guess she is not the talkative type," he said to his canine companion. He then entered the gate and made his way toward the woman. "Hello!" he said again.

This time, the woman stood up straight and briefly eyed him and the wolf before speaking back. "Hello," she said with a note of caution in her voice. Tara had seen many people come by her home on their way to the Royal City. Most were friendly enough, commenting on her flowers. Some were trying to sell her something and were cordial out of that necessity. However, this man and his wolf gave her a feeling of trepidation. Out of instinct, she rested her rake on the ground, holding it up between her and her unwelcomed visitors, "Is there something I can do for you?"

Jeru took note of her wary tone and decided to stop several cubits away from her so that she wouldn't feel so threatened by him, "I am trying to find some friends of mine. I have been trying to track them down for some time. It appears as though they may have passed this way. I wonder if you have seen them?" He said this in the kindliest tone he could muster. However, he had to wonder to himself if it sounded genuine at all. Kindliness was not a trait he had practiced in a long time.

In fact, to Tara, his question did not seem very sincere at all. She thought she could even detect a note of malice dripping off each word the man spoke. She answered the man as vaguely as possible, "I have been very busy in my garden today and haven't taken much notice of who was passing by." She hoped that would end the conversation and the man would move on.

Jeru was a bit annoyed by the cold tone and vagueness of her answer but decided to try again, "I understand that, but my friends would have been hard not to notice. You see, there would have had a giant man riding on the back of a behemoth in their group."

Tara tried again to be as evasive as she could. She thought that perhaps a bit of humor might break her growing tension, "As I said, I have been very busy here today. I probably wouldn't have noticed if a tree had walked by." She said this with a smile and pretended to return to her work to signal the end of the conversation.

Jeru decided he was finished with this foolishness and resorted to his usual tone, "Look, woman!" As he said this, he began to move closer to the woman. The wolf, picking up on the mood change, began to show his teeth and growl menacingly. "I know that they stopped here! You know that they stopped here! I only want to know how long ago that was and how many were with them. Just answer my questions, and I will move on!"

Tara had never been afraid of any animal before, but this wolf had a strange look in his eyes that she had never seen. She backed away slowly as she tried to think of an answer, "I...I think I may have seen them. I...I mean...so many people stop and look at my flowers. I don't always notice them. I do recall that a giant was with them now that I think about it. But, I am not sure how long ago that was." She swallowed hard, backing up slowly, her eyes oscillating between the man and the wolf.

Jeru could see the fear in the woman's eyes. Over the years, he had come to enjoy the sight of fear in people's eyes. It made him feel important; respected. He kept moving closer, "Now I'm starting to get some answers from you. I tried to be nice to you, but that didn't get me anywhere. I think it is better this way. We can now dispense with all the idle chit-chat. Now, how many of them were in the group, and who were they?"

Tara's mind raced. "I don't know. Perhaps there were seven or eight people, maybe ten. I did not count them. They said something about a wedding in the Royal City. I do not know anything more than that!"

Jeru eyed the woman for a few moments. He was satisfied that she had told him all she knew, but he wanted to feed off her fear for a little longer. He finally spoke again, "Was that so hard? You see? If you had only said that in the beginning, we could have avoided all this unpleasantness." He gave her a wry smile and pointed at her, "Remember this. If I ever need to question you again, just answer me. Do not try to be coy. I may not be as nice to you next time!" With that, he turned and walked calmly out of the garden and on toward the Royal City.

Tara watched him disappear out of sight before allowing herself to move. It was only then that she noticed her legs shaking. Her knees buckled, and they fell into the black earth beneath her. Through tears, she quietly prayed for the group of people she now felt as though she had betrayed. She also prayed for the man that was helping her in the garden earlier that day. She prayed that he would have wisdom in dealing with the trouble that was now coming his way.

Chapter 11

O NCE INSIDE THE KING'S RESIDENCE, THE WARY travelers were struck; not by the extravagance of a palatial estate with all the amenities of the wealthy but by the hominess of the place. In fact, Naamah thought that even her own home was decorated with more opulence than she saw here. There was finely crafted furniture and rugs in every room, and the stonework was the same inside as on the outside. However, none of it was so ornate as to give the impression that the king of the earth lived here. It was more utilitarian in nature.

Even the servants, if one could call them that, acted as if they were more a part of the family than royal subjects. In fact, as the guests were ushered into a dining hall, Adam was even scolded by one of them as he tried to sample a piece of fruit that was expertly arranged on a serving tray on one of the tables. He was reaching for it just as a rather rotund woman brought another tray into the room. "I see you!" she said. He only giggled and backed away as any child would have done if his mother had caught him doing the same.

The informality of the whole scene was not lost on Jaylon. He leaned over and whispered in Naamah's ear, "Who is in charge here, the servants or the masters?" Naamah had noticed his attitude change ever since they had picked up the stranger on the way into the city but decided not to address it now.

She only grabbed his hand and gently squeezed it. She herself was used to being shown a certain amount of respect by their servants at home but found the atmosphere of this place to be homey and quaint.

Before eating, Adam stood and asked the Lord's blessing on the food, not forgetting to bless the hands of the ones who had prepared it. Then, to Jaylon's continued amazement, the servants who were bringing out the food sat right down with them and began eating. Jaylon stared at them for a moment before shaking his head and whispering to himself, "Unbelievable." He looked around the room to see if anyone else was as shocked as he was. That was when he noticed Adam staring at him with a rather stern look in his eyes.

Now it was Jaylon who felt scolded. He had seen that look in the eyes of his own father. He suddenly felt like a child in trouble, only he did not know precisely why. He only looked down at his plate and ate the meal before him without another word.

Afterward, when everyone ate their fill and talked a bit more, Adam addressed the group, "I know you are all exhausted after your long journey." He then motioned toward one of the manservants standing in the doorway leading out of the hall, "Seelot here will show you to your rooms." The group stood and started following the servant. Jaylon could not wait to get to a place where he could unload his thoughts on his wife. He allowed her to take the lead but was caught gently by the arm before he could leave the room. He turned to see that it was Adam who had caught him.

Adam politely asked, "Jaylon, can I speak to you for a moment?"

Jaylon did not want to speak to him at that moment but agreed and turned back to his wife, "Naamah, I will be there soon."

Adam smiled at him, "Walk with me for a while." With that, he turned back through the hall and out another doorway. When he saw that they were sufficiently alone, his face turned more thoughtful, and he looked to the floor as he walked slowly with his fingers laced together. He began, "Jaylon, you seem troubled."

Jaylon thought for a moment before answering, "I don't know if "troubled" is the right word. I think "out of place" would be a better way to describe how I feel."

Adam pursed his lips together thoughtfully before speaking, "In what way do you feel out of place, my son?"

Jaylon tried to think of the best way to say what he wanted: "Where I live, I am considered an important man. I provide many jobs to the people of Urna in my emerald mines and my household. That being said, it is customary that I be treated with a certain amount of respect." At this point, he looked at Adam, who was still listening thoughtfully and continued, "Your customs here are very different than at home. My servants are not given the same respect as their master, they do not sleep in my home, and they certainly do not eat at the same table as my family, and I do. I feel they should know their place. They are not my equals. However, here in the Royal City, your servants act as if they are entitled to the same treatment as your guests. I find it to be a bit disturbing and strange. I suppose I'm used to more structure and order than that."

Adam did not speak for a few moments. Then, softly, he asked, "Jaylon, do you allow your children to eat at the table with you?"

Jaylon spoke quickly, "That is a different thing altogether. They are my children." Almost before the words left his mouth, he realized who he was speaking to, "I…I think I see what you are saying. However, I am not the Father of all the people on earth as you are. I am only the father of my two daughters."

Adam stopped and faced Jaylon with a gentle smile, "The Creator has entrusted you with the care of your two daughters, has He not?"

"Yes. I suppose He has," answered Jaylon.

Adam nodded in agreement, "Do you feel obligated to protect what the Lord has entrusted you with?"

Jaylon answered emphatically, "Of course, I would protect them. I would give my very life if need be!"

Adam nodded again, "Well said, Jaylon." He paused before continuing, "The Creator has also given you your own life. If you were in danger, would you protect yourself?"

Jaylon did not see where Adam was going with this line of questioning but answered anyway, "Yes. Of course, I would."

Adam restated the facts, "So, we have established that your life and the lives of your daughters and, I should add, the life of your wife, has been entrusted to your protection by the Creator of all life. Is that a fair statement?"

Jaylon nodded, "Yes."

"Tell me Jaylon, other than the fact that you own land where you found all those emeralds, is there anything special about you? Did the Creator give you an extra eye, an extra hand, or perhaps the ability to fly like a bird? Were you created any better than any of your servants?" Adam asked coolly.

Jaylon was struck by the absurdity of the question and answered flatly, "Of course not! I am no better than any of my servants!" He heard himself say it. He knew it was true at that moment, but it went against everything he had thought about himself before. The realization stopped him cold, and he turned to face a smiling Adam.

Adam softly spoke, "Jaylon, just as you have been entrusted with the lives of your family, you have been entrusted with those of your servants. You are no better than they. If the Lord had seen fit, He could have just as easily had you to be a servant of any of them. You see, although your servants are not your own children, they are His. He has entrusted you with their care. His intention was not that you lord your station in life over them. His intention was that you use the position he has blessed you with to protect them; to care for them; to love them as you love yourself; or, better yet, as He has loved you." Adam could see by the thoughtful look on Jaylon's face that his words had done their job.

———⟨ℐℐℐ⟩———

Time had gotten away from Eve and her new friend. After a long while of crying together and talking, Analeah told her the entire story. Eve had listened patiently while bouncing the playful Asham on her knee. As she heard of how Analeah had lost her firstborn son, Eve could not help but think of the loss of her first two sons.

Eve then gently touched Analeah's face, "Dear child, I know how difficult it was for you to tell me that. I thank you for trusting me enough to tell me the truth."

Analeah gave her a faint smile and looked to the ground as solemnity returned to her face, "It feels good to be able to un-load the burden on someone. I appreciate your understanding, but you must consider me a monster for what I have done. I understand. I think of myself the same way." She stood and reached out for Asham, "I thank you again for your time, but we should be going now."

Eve looked puzzled, "Child, where are you going?"

Analeah only shrugged her shoulders, her face awash in shame and self-condemnation, "You people have been so nice to me and my son. But I am unworthy of your company any longer now that you know what I am. We will go and find a place where no one knows us; a place where Asham will never have to know the shame of what his mother has done. I will always have to live with it, but it was not his fault. He shouldn't be burdened with it."

Eve looked directly into her eyes. Immediately, Analeah looked back to the ground. "Look at me, Daughter." Analeah slowly did so. "I know how you feel. You feel that no one could ever love you because of what you have done. The shame of it is constantly in your thoughts." At this point, Eve turned to look off into the distance before continuing, "I have done something that no one, least of all, myself, could ever forgive me for." Tears now started streaming down her face. "I have taken a precious gift from the Lord and discarded it. I traded it for a promise; a promise that only brought pain and shame."

Analeah knew that Eve was no longer speaking about what she had done. She was speaking from her own experience. She could see clearly the pain in her eyes. She allowed herself to feel someone else's pain for the first time in a long while. For those brief moments, she felt pity for someone other than herself. As she listened, tears welled up in her own eyes. A thought crossed her mind, "This woman might actually understand my pain better than anyone else on earth."

Eve continued, "I wanted to hide because I was exposed. I was suddenly aware of the horrible creature I was." After a moment, she looked back into Analeah's eyes, "You see Child, the decision I made all those years ago did not only cause pain for me and my husband. My selfishness made it possible for evil to flourish in this world. That one decision caused pain for everyone who came after me."

Eve bowed her head submissively to Analeah, "I am the one who caused all the pain in this world. You feel that I could never forgive you for what you have done, but in a very real sense, I am the one who did the greater evil. I am at fault for the death of your son." She looked back into Analeah's caring eyes with pleading eyes of her own, "Analeah, I do not fully understand how, but God has forgiven me for the most terrible sin anyone could ever commit. I ask you now, can you find it in your heart to forgive me for what I have done to you?"

Analeah felt so much love and compassion for her at that moment that she could barely speak. She only wrapped her arms tightly around Eve's quivering shoulders and spoke softly into her ear, "Yes!"

The two women clung to each other for a while before letting go and wiping their eyes. Eve put a hand on Analeah's knee, "Child, if the Lord can forgive me for what I have done, you need to know that He forgives you too. The real question is; will you forgive yourself? You will always feel the pain of what you have done. However, it is the pain of our bad decisions that teaches us to make better decisions later. Do you understand that?"

Analeah nodded, "Yes, I understand." After another moment, she took a deep breath, "I just wish others were as understanding as you are. What do I do now? You are so good to have listened to me and accepted me, but what will the others think of me when they learn what I have done?"

Eve laughed a little, "Sweet child, God has brought you here for a purpose. He has also chosen to acquaint you with some of the best people you will ever meet. I would be shocked if they reacted with anything other than the same love and acceptance that you have gotten from me. Come, let's go inside, get you and Asham something to eat, and find you a comfortable bed to sleep in. You must be starving and exhausted."

———•❧•———

Jeru had walked the winding road for a while, the light of day waning quickly. As he approached the gate leading in, he decided that a man and a wolf might cause undue attention. He opted to make camp under a large stand of oak trees a few hundred cubits off the road.

There, he formulated his plan. He would wait until morning, tie up the wolf, go into the city, and ask questions of some of the townspeople. "Surely," he thought, "it shouldn't take too long to find out where such a strange group of travelers had gone."

Chapter 12

AFTER A GOOD NIGHT'S SLEEP, THE GROUP STARTED milling about. Attracted by the smell of baking bread, they slowly assembled in the dining hall where they had eaten the night before. Eventually, Adam entered the room, followed by his wife, "Good morning! Everyone, find a seat, and breakfast will be served." He remained standing as everyone found their seats. He clapped his hands together cheerfully, "I trust we all had a good sleep."

Almost in unison, the entire group voiced their agreement. Ednah thought she would burst with curiosity if she didn't ask, "Will the King be joining us for breakfast this morning?" The whole group was anxious for the answer.

Adam laughed, "Lovely Ednah, I am sorry to disappoint you, but my son is a very early riser. He has already had his breakfast this morning. However, he is very anxious to meet you all and has requested an audience with everyone as soon as you have finished eating." The room was immediately filled with the sound of excited chatter at the news.

Adam continued as the servants began streaming in with platters filled with every kind of fruit and bread one could imagine, "Let us give thanks." The room got quiet, and all the servants stopped where they were and reverently bowed their heads. "Lord, we thank You for this bounty You have provided.

Help us to see Your provisions as a sign of Your love for each of us and, in turn, share that love with those around us. So be it!" With that, he clapped his hands again, "Let's eat!"

Concerned, Enoch asked, "Father Adam, would you mind if I took something out for Gardan?"

Adam laughed heartily, "Enoch, my son, why do you think the king is not with us? He could not wait to meet your giant friend. He chose to have his morning-meal with him."

Enoch smiled and nodded his understanding, "I should have already guessed."

Ednah could not contain herself, "Gardan got to meet him before any of us?!"

Enoch patted her hand, "I wouldn't say that." Confused, Ednah gave him a quizzical look. Enoch stopped her before she said another word, "Just eat your breakfast, Dear. You will understand soon enough." After a long stare and a huff, she did so.

Naamah, seated next to Ednah, leaned over and whispered into her ear, "It looks as though Naomi and Joaz have made themselves a friend." She said this as she nodded to where Eve was feeding the hungry boy on her lap, cooing over him. "Just look at Naomi smile! She looks like a new person this morning."

Ednah could not help but smile at the sight of it. "You are right. She does look like a new person. That is wonderful. I was beginning to worry about her."

Everyone ate heartily but quickly, anxious to meet the king. As they finished, they began assembling at the door into which they had entered. They milled about nervously, chatting, checking their clothing, and taking deep breaths to steady their nerves.

Seeing that everyone was finished, Adam stood and addressed the crowd, "If you would all follow me, I will take you to your audience." He graciously took Eve's hand and led the group through a side door. Seeing that they had all gathered at the wrong door, the group nervously giggled to each other, reassembled behind their guides, and filed out after them.

They went down a short hallway, around a corner, and into a small but well-adorned anteroom. This room was well furnished, with a few couches covered in beautifully woven, brightly colored fabrics. At the far end were broad, low, graduated steps leading up to a set of doors made of what appeared to be pure brass. On each side stood two very large and very armed men. Each held a small shield of the same brass as the doors. Their tunics were of a fine, dark blue, and around their waists were belts, which held finely polished swords on one side and equally fine daggers on the other. The guards' attire gave one the impression that they had never before had to soil themselves in battle. However, if the need ever arose, they would handle themselves quite capably.

Adam arched his back regally and asked them, "Is the king ready for his audience?" Without a word, they both nodded and reached over, opening their respective doors in unison.

Adam led Eve up the steps and into the room. The reverently silent crowd filed in two by two behind them into the most beautiful room that any of them had ever seen. The room's walls and floor were of the finest white and grey marble, polished to perfection. Though the entire room was only about twenty cubits wide and forty cubits in length, the clean, almost translucent marble gave the impression that it was much larger. At the far end of the room was a raised platform with what appeared to be four thrones of pure gold centered on it in a slight semicircle fashion. From the wall behind the thrones, cascading down from the platform, and all the way back to the entrance was a single rug. The fabric was red and blue, with pure gold threads woven throughout the piece.

The room was bright, despite the fact that it was window-less. This was due to the golden torches that hung at five cubit intervals down each wall. Behind each torch was a highly polished plate of pure silver that reflected the torchlight back into the room. It gave the effect of having no shadows anywhere to be seen.

However, as beautiful as this place was, everyone's attention was immediately drawn to the two thrones at the center of the platform. There sat a man and woman whose beauty made all the room's adornments pale in comparison.

The woman, obviously the queen, was dressed in a bright, blue-green dress that was so expertly embroidered with red and pink flowers that one would think they were real. The dress was bordered at every seam with a clean line of the same gold thread as the rug on the floor. Her skin was a dark olive tone, flawless and clean, while her hair was nearly pure black with only a few streaks of grey. It fell neatly down the edges of her face and over her shoulders to her waist. Her eyes were large and soft, bright and green. However, a gentle, welcoming smile seemed to emit more beauty than anything she wore.

The man to her left, however, was dressed in a tunic that was much more diffused in comparison to the queen's dress. It was obviously made of fine, soft fabric but of an eggshell color with dark brown borders. He was a very handsome man of muscular build and dark skin. His hair was greying a bit more than his queen's and fell naturally over his shoulders. However, as plain as his dress was, his bright blue eyes and wide smile seemed to exude an almost childlike excitement and jovial personality that threatened to outshine everything else in the room.

To a person, the onlookers were shocked at the sight of this man, the King of all the Earth. None were quite as shocked as Ednah and Jaylon, however. The dirty gardener they had met the day before was now seated on the throne before them.

King Seth could no longer hold his composure and bounced up and off the platform to greet his guests with hugs and slaps on their backs, "I know I shouldn't have tricked you all that way, but I just cannot seem to help myself!"

The queen stood and glided down the steps behind him to greet her guests in kind, "Please forgive my mischievous husband. He loves to play his little tricks on people." She came first to Ednah and gave her a welcoming hand, "You must be Ednah. Enoch has boasted many times about his lovely bride. I can now see why. I am so pleased to finally meet you."

Ednah blushed slightly at the compliment and bowed slightly, "My Queen, I am honored to meet you."

"Oh, come now!" said the queen. "We are family. Please call me Janis."

Ednah smiled humbly, "Janis."

The queen then put her arm around Ednah, turning her toward the rest of the group, "Now Ednah, please introduce me to your friends."

Eventually, all the introductions were made, save one. Eve had stayed close to Analeah and Asham, leading them around the room, out of the focus of attention. She then walked her up to the platform and stood facing the crowd, "If I may, I would like to make one last introduction." Everyone turned and faced Eve and her obviously nervous companion. "My new friend here would like me to tell you that she is sorry that she has deceived you as to her real name."

The group looked around at each other, a bit confused. Eve continued, "What she did, she did out of fear for her son. I believe once you hear her story, you will understand. So, in the meantime, I would like you all to meet Analeah and her son Asham."

Ednah and Naamah were still taken aback by the revelations and only looked at each other at first. King Seth and Queen Janis stepped forward and bowed slightly to their newly introduced guest. Queen Janis spoke first as she put an arm around her, "Welcome, Analeah. We are pleased to have you."

The King followed suit, "Yes, welcome, dear girl, to you and your son." He then took the queen's hand, walked her to her throne, and seated himself. At this point, the jovial smile had vanished and was replaced by a look of concern, "Analeah, my mother said that you were afraid for your son. Can you tell me why?"

With Eve's arm around her for support and with many tears, Analeah recounted the entire story for the king and queen as the rest of the guests listened along. By the time she was finished, there wasn't a dry eye in the assembly. Queen Janis and King Seth stood in unison. The queen went down to Analeah and embraced her caringly. At the same time, the king began pacing to and fro along the platform, clearly angry, his brow furrowed, rubbing his chin.

The king finally looked up and signaled for Enoch to join him on the platform. Enoch walked around the whole group of women who were now gathered around Analeah, trying to comfort her. The king spoke quietly to Enoch, "Enoch, I *cannot* allow this to continue! This Simyaza character *must* be made to pay for what he has done to those people." After a deep breath to steady his nerves and regain his composure, he continued, "I could use your council in this. What do you make of it all?"

"Well…" Enoch began, measuring his words, "As you know, eight years ago, I had dealings with another of his same ilk. She said that he appears to have some power over the health of their crops and livestock. That leads me to believe that we are dealing with a being of spiritual nature as much as physical." Enoch did a bit of pacing before returning to the king, "Please, allow me some time to pray about this before you make any decisions. I will need to take a walk alone for a while." Before leaving him, Enoch felt it necessary to tell the king what the Lord had already told him about the situation.

The king nodded his understanding, "Go. We will all pray for wisdom while you are gone."

Enoch then went to Ednah and whispered in her ear. She looked him in the eye and nodded in agreement. Enoch kissed her on the forehead and quietly left the room.

Only a few moments later, one of the heavily armed guards at the door came back through the door and made his way over to where the king was standing. He whispered something into his ear and waited for a response. "Go ahead and let her in," said the king. The guard bowed slightly, turned smartly on his heels, and returned, holding it open for Tara to enter.

Everyone in the room recognized her and became quiet and attentive to her arrival. The king addressed her directly, "Tara, my dear, what is troubling you today?"

Tara began nervously, clearly aware that everyone was listening, "My King, after you left my house yesterday, a man came along inquiring about your visitors here."

If the group wasn't paying attention before, they were now. The king asked his next question, "What sort of man was he, and what did he want to know?"

"Well, my King…" she began. "There was something… menacing about him. He tried to act nice about it at first, but there was something a bit… off about him. For one thing, he had a very large wolf with him. It was strange. I have seen wolves before, of course, but I had never seen one that I felt I needed to be afraid of."

Ednah had a hand on the shoulder of Analeah while the woman started talking but now noticed that she was trembling. She looked at her and saw that same expression of terror in her eyes that she had the day before, "What is it, Analeah?"

Through a quaky voice, she answered quietly, "They have found me!"

The king heard this and asked her directly, "Who, Analeah? Who has found you?"

Analeah answered through her hand, which was now over her mouth, "Simyaza's henchmen! They use the wolves to frighten people into doing what Simyaza wants."

King Seth was clearly confused by this. "I have never seen any animals intentionally try to hurt anyone before. How can it be that anyone would find them to be frightening?"

Tara said, "My King, I can vouch for what she says! I looked into the wolf's eyes yesterday. It meant me harm. It was plain to see."

The king shook his head, bewildered, "I see. Well, Tara, what was it that he wanted?"

"He wanted to know about these people, my King. He wanted to know when I saw them, how many there were, and where they were going. At first, I tried not to tell him anything, but he became very threatening. That wolf started growling at me, and I didn't know what to do, so I told him they were heading to the Royal City. I told him I didn't know anything more than that. He made another threat toward me and finally left. Last I saw him, he was heading this way. I felt that I should come and warn you." She looked back at Analeah and studied the terrified girl briefly before continuing, "I can only tell you that whatever he wants, it is not good."

———∿∿∿———

Enoch had exited the king's residence through a side door leading into an arboretum shaded by several different kinds of flowering vines. It was paved just as the courtyard was with all the colored stones and had several flower boxes from which the vines grew up and into the lattice through which the vines were woven. It seemed as though every color of creation was represented in the beautiful blooms surrounding him.

Enoch, however, had yet to notice any of this. His thoughts were squarely on the trouble at hand. He was deep in prayer, hands folded behind him as he made his way through the colorful labyrinth of greenery. He hardly even noticed a man working there until he had almost passed by him. The man was busy trimming a vine that had grown wildly out of place.

The man did not turn to look at him as he walked by, but Enoch was almost startled when the man spoke. "You know, when a gardener has a plan in mind for his garden, to see that plan come to fruition sometimes takes correction here and there."

A bit unaware that he was being spoken to for a moment, Enoch had to think about what the man said before replying, "Oh. Yes, I suppose it does." He had now stopped to see what the man was doing.

Still not turning to face Enoch, the man continued, "You see this vine? I have tried several times to weave it into the lattice here, but it insists on doing what it wants to. If only it would do what I had planned for it, it would thrive and be part of the beauty I have in mind for it. However, due to its unruliness, I am afraid that I am going to have to cut it away. I do not want to, but I cannot let it take over this whole area of my plan."

Enoch thought about what he was saying and agreed, "I suppose you are right. After all, you are the gardener."

It was only now that the man turned and looked directly at him. Enoch at once was shaken at the sight, "Lord! Forgive me for not recognizing you at once!" With that, Enoch went down on one knee out of reverence but also due to his legs losing their strength beneath him.

The Creator touched him on the shoulder, instantly bringing the strength back into his legs, "It is alright, My son. Stand up. We have much to discuss." He let Enoch get up and smiled at him. "Are you troubled by what Analeah has told you?"

Enoch shook his head, "I am very much troubled, Lord. Who is this Simyaza that he has such power over those people's crops and livestock?"

The Creator made a slight smirk, "Simyaza is, as you have already guessed, another like Azazel; one of the angels that were cast out of Heaven. He, like Azazel, has been given a task by his master, Lucifer. You see, when I created man, I took a very special interest in him. Everything you see; the trees, flowers, beasts, birds, and even the sun and moon, I spoke into existence. But man was different. I formed you out of the dust and breathed life into you. You were made in My own image. You are very special to Me.

"But, this made Lucifer very jealous. He was once the most beautiful of all My angels but, even he, in all his beauty, was only spoken into existence. It was when he realized that you were special, that I had given you My Spirit, that he became jealous and chose to defy Me. It was then that he decided to become the tempter that he is."

"Is he the reason then for all the trouble in the world?" Enoch asked.

The Creator shook his head, "Not exactly. I said he was the tempter, not the cause. You see, I created man with free will. The angels were created for the sole purpose of serving Me, but man was given a choice. I wanted man to *want* to serve and worship Me. Therefore, man also has the option of *not* serving and worshiping Me. That is where Lucifer decided to do his tempting.

"He is a liar; the father of lies. It is through his lies that he draws men into worshiping him instead of Me. He entices with empty promises that he cannot deliver. So, you see, he is not the cause of all the evil in the world. He only tempts man into doing the evil themselves."

Enoch was puzzled, "Then, how does he have the power of life and death over the crops and livestock of the people in Baalta?"

The Lord stopped and faced Enoch directly, "He only has the power that the people who choose to worship him have given him. Remember, he is the father of lies. If they focus only on what he tells them, they will be given over to his illusions. If those people choose to put their faith in him, they will reap the consequences: empty promises, curses, barrenness, and death. If they choose, as you have, to put their faith in Me, they would reap much different results."

Enoch still had a question, "How, then, can this Simyaza have the ability to take their children and sacrifice them?"

"Enoch," He said slowly and firmly. "He does not have that ability unless it is given to him. Those children were not *taken* from them. They were *given* to Simyaza. The parents had a choice. They could have simply said 'no.' Instead, they freely gave their children to Simyaza for the promise of having his blessings. Simyaza's mission is not to destroy those people. It is to tempt them into destroying themselves."

Enoch's mind was reeling. The revelation of what he was told shook him to the core. He thought about all the evil he had ever seen or heard about and realized that it was done by the people who chose to do it. At some point in every instance, a choice was made. Enoch gathered his thoughts again and asked his final question, "What shall we do now?"

The Lord smiled at him and answered, "You will know what to do when the time comes. Just remember, put your faith in Me. Do not rely on your own understanding. When it looks as though all hope is lost, My timing is perfect."

Enoch blinked his eyes, and the Creator was gone. He took a deep breath, offered a prayer of thanks, and turned back toward the king's residence.

Chapter 13

J ERU'S MORNING HAD NOT GONE WELL. HE WOKE TO find that the small loaf of bread he had brought and was saving for his breakfast had been almost entirely devoured by a large colony of huge ants. The fact that he had stored that loaf securely in the tunic he was wearing was perhaps the most disturbing thing. Upon opening his eyes, he realized he was covered in the creatures. Until now, they had found no reason to bite him, but with his sudden jump, subsequent swiping, and slapping, not to mention his lively little dance, they found a good reason to start.

It took him a little time to deal with, but eventually, he settled down and regained his composure. He decided to tie his wolf in another area of the oak hammock and return to the road that led into the city. He thought he would just enter the Royal City and find something to eat while asking around about his quarry.

As he approached the road, he caught a glimpse of a woman walking briskly toward the city gate. He stopped behind a large tree and watched quietly as she passed by. He smiled derisively when he realized it was the same woman he had harassed the day before. "I'll just follow her. She will lead me right to them," Jeru thought to himself.

He kept his distance, nonchalantly meandering through the city, pretending to take an interest in the sights. When she approached a large residence surrounded by an elaborately manicured courtyard, he stopped across the thoroughfare at a small stand selling fruits and cakes. There, he kept watch and bought his breakfast.

He saw her approach a worker who was busy pruning the flowers in one of the many boxes that covered the courtyard and speak to him. A moment later, the worker pointed and led her to the door, where they quickly entered the large house. He thought to himself, "So, that is where they went."

He decided to slowly make his way around the residence and see what there was to see. He calmly ate his breakfast, noting that it tasted a bit off. He had been used to the bread of Baalta and thought the cake he was eating now to be tasteless and nearly spoiled. However, he was hungry and continued eating as he strolled slowly and deliberately, making a wide circle around the large house. He eventually made his way halfway around and suddenly realized his path was blocked, and the sight of what blocked his way made him stop in his tracks.

He stood wide-eyed, looking at the largest man he had ever seen, who was standing next to an even larger behemoth. The giant man rubbed the behemoth and spoke softly to it as though it were his pet. He took special note of the fact that the colossal man wore an enormous sword at his side. It took some time to get over the initial shock of what he was seeing before he regained his wits and decided to return to the front of the estate.

This was where his morning took a real turn for the worse. As he was coming to the front corner of the house, a woman suddenly appeared flanked by two very big, well-armed guards. His attention, of course, was immediately drawn to the guards, who were dressed in very sharp-looking uniforms and adorned with equally sharp-looking swords. Only when the woman pointed directly at him did he realize who she was—the woman he had followed into the city!

He stood stock still for a moment. His mind raced, and his eyes widened to take in the sight of the guards, who were quickly filling his entire view. By the time his feet finally got the message to move, it was too late. The guards were already upon him.

⚬⚬⚬

As Enoch entered the throne room from the side door he had exited earlier, the double doors opened wide to reveal the two guards dragging a whimpering little man into the room. The whole assembly parted to either side to allow them to bring the distraught man to the front of the platform where the king and queen were seated. Tara followed behind.

The king shook his head as he addressed Tara, "Dear woman, you didn't waste much time in finding him, did you?"

Tara glared at the sniveling man, "He made it easy, my King. He was only just outside, skulking about."

The guards held the man by both arms when Jeru started to hiss, "Who do you think..." In one smooth movement, the guard on his left had pulled his dagger and brought it around, expertly jabbing the point behind the man's left knee, causing him to assume a more respectable kneeling position. Jeru yelped as he landed with a thud on the unforgiving marble.

The king narrowed his eyes at him and leaned forward on his throne, "Who do I think I am? Is *that* what you were about to ask me?" He didn't wait for a response. "I am Seth, King of the Earth. Who do you think *you* are?"

Jeru blinked for a moment. He started to spout a boastful answer, but it only came out as a whimper, "I...I am Jeru; a servant of Simyaza; Governor of Baalta."

The king had to fight back a snicker at the weak way the man had answered, "Do you realize, Jeru, servant of Simyaza, I could have you executed for treating my friend, Tara, the way you did?" The king had never had to give such an order before and, truth be told, despised the thought of shedding blood. However, he thought the mere threat of it would play nicely upon the man's apparent fear.

Jeru opened his mouth to answer but found that the weight of the king's statement left him silent. The king continued, "What is your business here?"

Jeru finally found his words, "I was sent to retrieve the property of a citizen of Baalta. His wife has run away with his son."

The king now sat back in his seat and spoke a bit more softly, "You speak of this man's wife and son as 'property?' Is *that* how this man sees his family, that he would send a servant out to retrieve them as if they were merely a pair of oxen? Why didn't the man come here himself?"

Jeru's dislike for Jotham came through easily in his answer, "The man is weak and stupid! I do not even *blame* the woman for leaving him, but I was given the task to find them and bring them back. I am only doing what I was told."

"This 'Simyaza,' who *claims* to be Governor, told you to find them?" asked the king with obvious derision. "Why would the Governor of Baalta be so concerned that a woman would leave a 'weak and stupid' man, as you say he is? Why are she and her son so important to this 'Simyaza' character?"

Jeru spouted his answer without thinking, "Simyaza doesn't allow anyone to leave!" He instantly realized he should have answered differently, but the king had already seized upon the answer.

"Simyaza doesn't '*allow*' anyone to leave Baalta? What gives him authority over anyone's choices as to whether they come or go as they please?" The king now shifted forward in his seat again. "What is he so afraid of? Is there something that he doesn't want anyone to know about?"

Jeru only looked to the floor silently. The king's voice regained its more forceful quality, "I do not require an answer from you, you *weak* little man! I have already heard about what has been happening in Baalta!" The anger in his voice almost shook the room, "I have heard about the sacrifices of children to this *Simyaza*! You asked me who I think *I* am. Well, you tell me! Who does he think *he* is to ask people to sacrifice their children to *him*?"

At this point, the king could not sit any longer. He stood and paced the platform, his voice deep and menacing, "I will agree with you on one note. This man for whom you are retrieving his '*property*' is weak and stupid! Anyone who would allow his own child to be killed to appease such a man as this, Simyaza, is not worth his own *skin*! Much less is he worthy of a wife and *another* child. As far as I am concerned, he no longer has any *rights* to that wife and child. He gave up those rights along with his *spine*!"

The king calmed slightly but now leveled his eyes at Jeru, "Also, you putrid little man, *anyone* who would do the bidding of a man like Simyaza is a waste of his *own* skin!" The king now addressed the guards, "Take him out of this house! The stench of him offends my queen and my guests. Bind him hand and foot and lie him face down in the soil like the snake he is until I decide what to do with him." With that, Jeru was unceremoniously dragged from the room.

The king took a deep breath before speaking again, "Enoch, Jaylon, Methuselah, and Jubal, I would like your counsel on this matter." He then turned to the queen and put a loving hand on her leg, speaking gently, "My Queen, would you please see that the others are made comfortable while we discuss this terrible business?"

The queen nodded and stood, making her way down from the platform and toward the door leading out to the arboretum. "I would like to show you our gardens. We have collected the most beautiful flowers from all the earth. Please follow me." With that, the group of women silently followed.

The king waited for their exit, then addressed the men, "I would like to include my new friend, Gardan, in this discussion also. If this man, Simyaza, is what I think he is, I believe Gardan will have some unique insight on all of this." The men nodded their agreement and followed the king through a door at the rear of the throne room.

The six men gathered outside the stables under the sprawling limbs of an enormous oak tree where there were chairs and a table. The men found a seat while Gardan sat, leaning against the trunk of one of the oaks. The king began by recounting the entire story to Gardan, the emotions still evident in his voice. Clearly, the more Gardan learned, the more agitated he got until he found himself on his feet, pacing around and wrenching his enormous hands.

The king finished, "And now, my large friend, you know what we know. I want your council on this matter, along with the rest of these men. I believe your insights might prove helpful."

Gardan stopped pacing and took a deep breath, looking thoughtfully through the trees as if staring into the past. He spoke softly, yet there was no mistaking the disgust in his voice, "I know well who Simyaza is. He is one like my father, a Fallen One." The other men exchanged glances with each other as Gardan continued, "I met him once when I was just a boy. He came to see my father. I do not know what was said, but it was easy to see that they had some sort of rivalry."

Gardan rubbed his face and shook his head, "That is all I know of him. However, I believe there are some things that can be inferred. My father was a purely evil sort. He never did anything good. His sole purpose, as I saw it, was to destroy as many people as possible by teaching them how to make war with each other." He looked directly at the king, "His progress is clearly evident by the fact that your own guards are armed with the very swords he taught men to make."

The king's face showed a disturbing look of revelation. He pursed his lips, looked to the ground, and shook his head, "Gardan, you shame me. I suppose I have, in essence, done exactly what your father wanted."

Gardan put a hand up while putting the other hand on the hilt of his own massive sword, "My King, do I not wear the same weapon at my side? What I said was not meant to shame you. I was only pointing out the fact that our adversaries are very crafty and adept at their work. My father may have given men the ideas. However, once that was done, man's own aptitude for evil did the rest." Gardan now slapped at the hilt of his sword. "No, I am afraid that once the evil men of the earth started using these weapons for evil purposes, it forced the good men to adapt in order to stop them. This appears to be the cycle of things."

The king nodded as he looked at his large friend with new-found appreciation, "Gardan, my giant friend, you have much wisdom. So, tell me, if that was what your father's task, what do you see in the actions of Simyaza?"

Gardan thought for a moment, "I couldn't tell you with any assurance exactly *what* he is up to. However, the basics remain the same. He is doing the same thing, only using different tactics. He is using people's aptitude for evil to get them to destroy themselves."

The king looked to the other men at the table, who nodded their agreement, "Well said, Gardan."

Methuselah now spoke up, "If that is so, it seems to me that we are not merely fighting against Simyaza. We will be fighting against the people that are under his influence as well. We know, of course, that we are on the side of good in this, but will we not be playing into the very thing that Gardan's father and, apparently, Simyaza wants? We will be destroying each other."

The king looked for a long moment at the young man before addressing Enoch, "Enoch, your son has inherited much more from you than your physical features." Methuselah blushed a bit at the compliment.

Jaylon now spoke, "If I may, my King, it would seem to me a foolhardy venture to raise an army to march on a walled city. There would be much bloodshed on our side before we could even get within their gates. Even at that, given the situation, are not the people of Baalta only being used by Simyaza? Perhaps there is a way they could be persuaded that they are being deceived."

The king thought about what Jaylon had said and agreed, "You are right, my friend. I would like to avoid any unnecessary bloodshed. How do *you* propose that we handle it?"

Jaylon thought momentarily and measured his words carefully, "Perhaps we could use a diplomatic approach first. If you send an army in, swords drawn, the outcome will be sure either way; there will be much blood spilled. However, a small delegation of statesmen armed with words instead of swords might have a better chance of making known your feelings on the matter without any bloodshed. After that, you would, at least, be able to make a more informed decision as to the best plan of action. If a full-scale attack is still necessary, you would then have the benefit of knowing the layout of the city, its strengths, and weaknesses."

The king smiled widely at Jaylon, "It appears that I have chosen my councilmen well. That is a very good idea." He then looked at Enoch, "Enoch, you have been very quiet. I would very much value your thoughts on the matter. It is no secret that the Creator speaks to you directly. At a time such as this, it is *His* thoughts that are most important."

Enoch was quiet and thought before answering, "The Lord only told me to rely on Him. He said that I would know what to do when the time came. However, I feel that Jaylon's advice is sound. We need only to decide who will make up the delegation. The Lord *has* said that Methuselah and I are to go. He did not tell me anything other than that. I believe that any other members of our party should be decided prayerfully. I have the feeling that this journey could be fraught with dangers. Let us decide wisely."

Jubal interjected, "I am more than willing to come along and watch your backs. If the townspeople are loyal to Simyaza, it is possible they would attempt to harm our delegation… or *worse*! You saw for yourselves what kind of people they are when Simyaza's spy was caught. Going in peacefully may be the wise thing to do, but I believe there is also power in numbers. And, if Gardan was with us, they would *never* think to try harming any of us!"

Gardan put a gentle hand on Jubal's shoulder and spoke thoughtfully, "Jubal, I appreciate your loyalty, and there is a certain amount of wisdom in what you say. However, I'm afraid my presence would do more to foster confrontation than avoid it. Simyaza, no doubt, has heard of my role in what happened in Urna eight years ago. He and my father may be rivals, but they have the same master. I believe my being there would be seen as a direct threat, and Simyaza would think nothing of forcing the townspeople to attack. That, in turn, would force me to defend all of you. The *last* thing I want to do is to be the *cause* of bloodshed!"

Enoch agreed, "Jubal, I think Gardan is right. A show of strength is tantamount to a threat of violence. If we find that to be necessary, so be it. However, I truly think a peaceful visit would give us a better chance to assess the situation." Enoch looked around the group and smiled at them all, "The Lord has asked Methuselah and I to go. If He wanted anyone else to go, He would have said so. However, I would greatly appreciate the chance to pray together for our success and safe return."

With that, all six men went to their knees and sought the Lord's blessing on the plan. Enoch pleaded for wisdom, discernment, and courage for what lay ahead. While listening to the others pray, Enoch heard another Voice softly whisper, "Seth needs to release Jeru and allow him to return to Baalta. Remember, trust Me and allow *Me* to be your Shield. I will do a great work through your weakness."

Chapter 14

RONIN AND JOTHAM HAD GOTTEN BACK TO BAALTA very late in the evening. They decided to get some sleep and speak with Simyaza early the next morning. As they entered Simyaza's house, they were met by Simyaza's sickly-looking servant, Telah. "Wait here," Telah said as he turned and disappeared into another room. He soon returned and announced, "Master Simyaza will see you now. Follow me."

The men followed him into the next room, where Simyaza stared at them menacingly. "Where is Jeru?" Simyaza growled.

Fearful of his tone, Ronin stuttered as he answered, "W… We followed the woman's scent for a long distance. It appears that she is a crafty woman. She left the city through the livestock gate and went through the countryside rather than taking the roads. It took a while to get her direction, but we were finally able to track her through the farmlands. She is quite cunning. She…"

"I do not want to hear any more about how crafty or cunning she is!" Simyaza barked. "I asked you a question! Where is Jeru?"

Jotham couldn't help a satisfied smirk as he watched Ronin squirm. "I told him the same thing, Simyaza! He and Jeru kept saying…"

"Did I ask you to speak?" Simyaza growled. This elicited a smirk from Ronin.

Ronin spoke up again, "My apologies, Master. If I may continue, I believe you will find the rest of my story quite interesting." Simyaza rolled his eyes and his boney-fingered hand to signify that he should get on with it. Ronin nervously continued, "Well, we tracked her to a lake near the road leading to the Royal City. It was clear that she had stopped and slept there for the night. That was where we lost her trail."

Simyaza was clearly agitated now, "You lost her trail! What do you mean, you lost her trail?"

Ronin nodded, "Y...Yes, we lost her trail, but she was obviously picked up by some travelers. That is what was so interesting. The travelers had several carriages. We found the tracks of horses and oxen along with their wheel tracks, but there were other tracks there too. It looks as if the travelers had a giant with them; a giant who was riding a behemoth as if it were a horse. I have heard stories..."

"Gardan!" spat Simyaza.

"Gardan, Master?" Ronin asked. "Who is Gardan?"

Simyaza stroked his chin slowly now, speaking more to himself than answering Ronin's question, "Gardan is the idiot son of someone I have had dealings with before. I had heard that he was living among the people of Urna now. I have also heard that he had become a close friend of *Enoch*." Simyaza almost spat Enoch's name when he said it. He now directed another question to Ronin, "Did the tracks indicate that they were headed toward the Royal City or away from it?"

Ronin answered, "They were headed toward the Royal City. That is where Jeru is now. I thought it best if one of us followed the tracks to see what they were up to, while the other reported what we found back to you. I thought that you..."

"I do not want to hear what *you* thought!" Simyaza interrupted. "What plan did your tiny minds devise from there?"

Ronin looked to the floor, a bit embarrassed by Simyaza's insult, "I was going to let you advise me as to what to do and meet Jeru back at the lakeside tomorrow."

Simyaza stroked his chin again as he thought about the situation, "Go and meet him as planned. Then return to me with any information you have. Go now! Do not waste any time. I want to hear from you as soon as possible."

With that, Ronin turned on his heels and left the house. Jotham watched him go and turned back to Simyaza, "What about my son? When will I get my son back? You said…"

"I said," Simyaza spouted vociferously, "I would help you get your son back! You must have patience. The situation has taken an unexpected turn, but you must trust me." Simyaza now eyed him cruelly. "Do you doubt my word, Jotham?"

Jotham answered nervously, "No, Simyaza. Never!" He was secretly asking himself the same question Simyaza had just asked him.

—⋘◈⋙—

Enoch brought up the other part of the Lord's directive, "King Seth, the Creator said that you should allow Jeru to go free."

The king was incredulous. He only stared at Enoch for a long moment before replying, "Are you sure that is what He said, Enoch? The man has already proven himself to be dangerous. You know he will only help our enemy, don't you?"

Enoch lightly shrugged his shoulders, "That may be, my King. However, the Lord was clear about it. You are to let him go. I have, over the years, come to realize that the Creator does not make mistakes. If I lean solely on my own understanding, it does not take me very long to make a mess of things. It is only when I put all my trust in Him and what He says that things tend to work for the good."

The king thought about what Enoch said before he finally conceded, "Of course, Enoch. You are right." He called to a guard who was standing several cubits away, "Latham! Have the man, Jeru, untied and brought to me." The guard only nodded and disappeared. The king turned his attention back to Enoch and Methuselah, "When would the two of you like to leave?"

Enoch and Methuselah exchanged a glance of understanding before Methuselah spoke up, "My King, I would like to have some time to explain the situation to Tamari before we leave." Methuselah then looked to the ground in contemplation while speaking more to himself than anyone else, "I only hope that she will understand that our wedding must be postponed until we return."

The king was suddenly troubled and put an understanding hand on the young man's shoulder. "I am sorry, my son. I believe, in the confusion of the day's events, the entire reason for your visit to the Royal City was forgotten. Please, forgive me."

Methuselah put up a hand and gave a slight smile to the king. "My King, there is no forgiveness necessary. It is true that my understanding for this visit was that you would do the honor of conducting my wedding. However, through the teaching of my father, I have learned that the Lord's plans are not always the same as ours. It is apparent to me that the entire reason for our visit was not my wedding. As important as that is to me, I must submit myself and my wants to His will. I believe the Creator will honor that. If I honor Him, He will bless me and give me the desires of my heart."

The king looked at Methuselah for a long while before speaking, "Methuselah, you are your father's son. Your wisdom at such a young age almost shames me."

For the last eight years, Jaylon had come to realize that Methuselah was a fine young man. However, in the last few moments, he had come to realize just how much integrity he possessed. He put his arm around him, a simple gesture that was not lost on Methuselah.

Then, the guard appeared again with the disheveled Jeru, hands bound behind him and soil all over his front side after being tied face-down in the dirt. Jeru said nothing. The look on his face said enough as he only scowled at the king as they approached.

The king spoke to the guard but never looked anywhere but directly into Jeru's eyes, "Release him."

The guard was a bit confused by the order, but his confusion was nothing compared with the shock that came across the face of Jeru. The guard cocked his head sideways and asked, "Release him, my King?"

The king repeated his order, "Release him." The guard did as he was told, producing a dagger and cutting Jeru's ropes. Jeru kept staring at the king while he momentarily wrung his sore wrists. His lips parted for an instant as if he was going to say something, but he quickly shut them and backed up slowly before turning completely away. His pace quickened until he disappeared around a corner and out of sight.

After watching this, Enoch could see that the king was troubled. He decided that perhaps the king needed a few moments to himself. He lightly slapped Methuselah on the back, "Well, Son, we had better go speak with the women. I think we will both have some explaining to do." Methuselah took a deep breath and nodded his agreement.

—◦◦◦—

"This is *supposed* to be our *wedding*! How can you ask me to postpone our wedding? I don't understand why *you* have to go! What am I supposed to do if something happens to you, Methuselah?" Methuselah somehow knew there was no good answer to that last question and decided to keep quiet. Tamari was pacing around the room with her hands on her hips.

Methuselah loved her so much and knew that she would eventually calm down. It wasn't in Tamari's nature to stay angry very long. In fact, it was so out of place for her to be so angry that Methuselah had to fight back a snicker or two during her tirade. He even had a hard time listening to what she was saying because he found her to be so beautiful, even with her brows furrowed, her lips pursed, and stomping around the room.

After a while, she was spent and remained quiet, standing at the other end of the room, looking down at her feet. She finally took a deep breath and let her hands fall from her hips. She turned back to Methuselah, her expression a little softer now. She even managed a slight smile. "I suppose you think I am being a child about this."

Methuselah gave her a wide grin and approached her, putting his arms around her and looking her deep in the eyes, "You do not look like a child to *me*." He gently kissed her forehead, and she nestled into his strong arms. They remained there for a long while as Methuselah slowly caressed her back. Realizing the intensity of the embrace, they pushed away and put some distance between them. They both spent a few silent moments blushing before regaining their composure.

Tamari spoke first, "So, when do you plan to leave?"

Methuselah cleared his throat before answering shyly, "I think…I think we will leave today. I hope to be able to get back as soon as possible…so, I hope to leave soon."

Tamari now blushed a bit at his answer. They had been planning this wedding for eight years now. It seemed like an eternity to both of them, as it often does with young people who are so madly in love. She regained her typical playfulness, "You had better get back to me soon! I may decide that I am tired of waiting and go back home."

Methuselah smiled widely, "I suppose I better hurry back. Too long, and I may forget what you look like." They both gave a nervous giggle. However, as they looked at each other, their smiles slowly morphed into more somber expressions. Methuselah then spoke clearly and slowly in all seriousness, with none of his usual humor, "I love you."

—◦◦◦—

Jeru had wasted no time in making his retreat. He quickly went out through the city gate and found his wolf lying where he had left him in the oak hammock near the road. He walked briskly down the road, past the gardened cottage, and eventually found himself nearing the lake where he was to meet with Ronin. He had brushed off all the soil from his tunic and washed his face in a stream near the road.

He had decided that Ronin did not need to know the whole story. He would simply tell him he had met with the king, made his claim on Jotham's property, and that the king had the audacity to deny him that claim. Nothing else needed to be said.

As he approached the lake, he was prepared to spend the night there awaiting his appointment with Ronin. To his surprise, he saw Ronin approaching from the other direction. Jeru went out to meet him and told him the story, at least as much as he felt Ronin needed to know.

The two men decided to head for Baalta. They now had something solid to report to Simyaza.

Chapter 15

AFTER SECURING DIRECTIONS TO BAALTA, ENOCH and Methuselah were on their way. The king had loaned them one of his more stately, smooth-riding carriages, and the only sound for a long time was the clip-clop of the horses' hooves on the hard-packed road. Both men had things on their minds which took them a while to organize and think clearly about.

Enoch was meditating on what the Lord had said about knowing what he should do when the time came. He had practiced this for many years and, from experience, knew that everything would work out for the good in the end. However, looking at it from hindsight was one thing. He had a good grasp of right and wrong; this foundation had always informed him well in his decisions. Still, the pressure of expectations— of making the right decision in a matter of the unknown and unpredictable—was a different thing altogether.

Methuselah's thoughts were of a similar nature. He was completely aware of his inexperience. He had always thought of himself as a simple farmer. If someone had told him two days ago that he would be part of a delegation going into what was likely to be enemy territory on behalf of the King of the Earth, he would have questioned their sanity. However, here he was. He was thankful that he had his father's experience to rely on and had already resigned himself to following his lead. Still, the fear of the unknown was invading his thoughts. Every time the weight of their mission came to mind, his heart sank underneath it.

As they passed Tara's cottage and he stared at the brilliant flowers surrounding it, Methuselah took a deep breath and voiced his thoughts, "Father, why do you suppose the Lord wanted me to come along on this delegation? Please, do not misunderstand me. I am not questioning the Lord. There must be a good reason for it, but it seems that Jaylon would be more experienced and better equipped to deal with matters of such importance."

Enoch thought for a moment before answering. Truth be told, he had the same thought. "My son, you are right. Jaylon has indeed had a lot of experience in negotiating in his business. He has been blessed with a level head when faced with disagreeable situations. However, I suspect that it has not always been so. As you yourself have seen, his temper has, in the past, gotten the best of him. It has only been through those very years of experience, and the help of the Lord, that he has learned how to control that temper and make better decisions. Perhaps the Lord wants you to learn something through this experience."

Methuselah thought about his father's words, "I suppose you are right. I have seen a big change in him over the last eight years. I just worry that I might do something wrong, that I will say something wrong and cause the Lord to regret His decision to send me to Baalta with you."

Enoch had to laugh a bit at that, "My son, if there is anything I know about the Lord, He does not make bad decisions. As you have said, there must be a good reason for your being here. Just trust Him in all things, and you will know what to do when the time comes." Enoch saw the irony in what he had said almost before the words left his mouth. He had the same worries as his son, yet he found himself giving the same advice that he had been given. He chuckled to himself, "I have given you good advice. We both should follow it."

They rode along for a while longer before recognizing that they were approaching the lakeside where they had picked up Analeah and Asham the day before. The sun was descending, and it wouldn't be long before they made it to the place where they would be turning toward Baalta. From there, reaching their destination would only take about half a day. Enoch decided it would be a good idea if they stopped at the lake and camped for the night. Methuselah agreed.

As the horses grazed on the lush green grass surrounding the lake, the two men had a quiet supper of bread and fruit and bedded down for the night. Sleep came slowly but eventually replaced their heavy thoughts.

＝＝＊＊＊＝＝

Night had only just fallen by the time Ronin and Jeru reached Baalta. They made their way to Simyaza's house. They were coldly welcomed in the usual way by Simyaza's servant, Telah, "Follow me. Master Simyaza has been expecting you." They did so.

As they entered the room, Simyaza was sitting in an over-sized chair facing away from them, staring into the fire in the large stone hearth. Without turning, he spoke in even, flat tones, "You have news for me?"

Ronin looked at Jeru and nodded for him to answer. Jeru stuttered as he began, "Y-yes, Master Simyaza, I do. I followed the tracks that Ronin told you about. They led me to the Royal City. Actually, they led me directly to the residence of King Seth." Jeru waited to see if there would be any response.

Simyaza still did not move. "Go on," he said flatly.

Jeru looked nervously at Ronin before continuing, "Well, before I got to the Royal City, I saw that the caravan had stopped at a woman's house. I decided I would question her about them. She would not answer me, so I threatened her until she did. She finally told me what I wanted to know, but…"

His hesitation finally elicited a livelier response from Simyaza, "But, what?"

Jeru swallowed hard, "But, by the time I got to the Royal City, it was getting dark and decided to wait until morning to go in. I camped in an oak hammock near the city gates. The next morning, I saw the woman walking by and followed her right to the king's residence. She went inside for a while, so I had a look around. Behind the house, near the stables, I saw a giant man tending to a behemoth! Simyaza, he was enormous! He…"

Simyaza suddenly stood and spun to face the man, "I do not care how big the man was! I only want to know what you learned!"

Jeru stammered and looked to the floor as he continued, "Well, when I went back around toward the front of the house, that woman came around the corner with two of the Royal guards. Before I knew it, she pointed me out and the guards grabbed me and forced me inside. I tried to run, but they were too close. They…"

"You *oaf*!" Simyaza spat. "You allowed them to *catch* you?"

Jeru stammered again, "They were upon me before I knew it, Master! I couldn't get away."

Simyaza calmed a bit. "But it appears as though you managed to get away somehow. How did you accomplish that?"

Jeru took the opportunity to try and make himself look a little better, "I just told the king that I was there to retrieve the property of one of your subjects, and that he should not interfere with that." Jeru now took on an air of superiority, sticking out his chin for added effect, "I said, 'I represent

Simyaza, Governor of Baalta, and he wants back what right-fully belongs to him!'"

Simyaza stood and approached him slowly, "Is that what you told him, Jeru?"

Jeru proudly answered, "Yes. That is what I told him."

Simyaza put his long, slender fingers around Jeru's shoulder and smiled at him while he asked his next question, "And, what did the king say when you told him that?"

Jeru was now starting to feel uncomfortable at Simyaza's touch. He could feel a cold, sick emanation traveling from his shoulder and down his spine. He tried to keep his composure as he answered, "H…he said that the woman and her child were no longer yours to claim. He said that they were now under his protection and ordered me to leave. I protested, but he threatened me with execution and I left."

Simyaza kept the smile on his face while he tightened his grip on Jeru's shoulder. "He said that the woman and her child were no longer mine to claim?" Jeru was starting to wince in pain. "They are now under his protection?" Jeru's legs were now starting to buckle as the pain intensified. "He then threatened you with execution unless you left?" Jeru now fell to his knees while grasping vainly at Simyaza's hand, trying to loosen his viselike grip on his shoulder.

Simyaza's expression never changed. His strength seemed effortless as he continued to smile at Jeru. Ronin took a few steps back, repulsed by the sounds of bones snapping. "You should have let him kill you because what I have in mind for you will be much worse." Simyaza continued to smile as Jeru's body went limp. He had passed out from the pain. Simyaza released his grip, and Jeru's body folded to the floor.

Ronin looked nervously at Simyaza, who was now eyeing him. Simyaza never changed his expression, "Was there anything else to report?"

Ronin's voice shook slightly as he kept his distance and answered, "Jeru told me that the king seemed to know about the sacrifices. He said that he was outraged. He may be sending someone to investigate. I would not be surprised if he did."

Simyaza stroked his chin and slowly paced around the room, "The woman must have told him. I am sure he will send someone to investigate." A smile came over his face again. "I would wager whom he shall send, Enoch!" Simyaza now laughed and clapped his hands as his dark eyes twinkled with excitement, "This is going to be interesting!"

Simyaza looked back to the floor where a groaning Jeru was starting to regain consciousness and barked at Ronin, "Get that fool out of here! Tell him he would be wise to keep his distance from me for a while."

Chapter 16

*I*T WAS PITCH-DARK. METHUSELAH COULD ONLY make out the small form of a child illuminated by a single shaft of moonlight. The child was lying on a soft blanket in a stone trough, looking up at him, cooing, and waving his hands as a child does when he is very young. Methuselah smiled at it and spoke softly, "What are you doing here, Little One?"

He did not know what to make of it until he sensed a dark figure approaching from somewhere to his left. He turned to see who it was but could not. The darkness was too heavy. He could only sense the evil presence that accompanied it. "Who are you? What do you want?" Methuselah asked but got no answer.

Then, he saw the blood-stained blade of a sword move upward through the shaft of moonlight directly above the child. His mind raced. He knew that if the blade returned down in the same direction, it would cut the child in half. Instinctively, he jumped between the assailant and the child and yelled, "In the name of the Lord, no!"

———⊰⊱———

"In the name of the Lord, no!" Methuselah yelled.

Both men sat straight up. Enoch looked over at Methuselah, who returned a look of terror. "Methuselah, what is the matter? Are you alright?"

Methuselah wiped his face and rubbed his eyes. He had only been dreaming. He looked around and could see the lake and the fig trees surrounding it. It was early morning, and the sun had not yet made its appearance over the horizon, but the coming light was evident in the sky above. He rubbed his eyes again before answering his worried father, "I am alright, Father. I was just having a dream."

Enoch stared at him momentarily and rubbed his eyes, "It was not a pleasant dream, I take it?"

Methuselah looked out at the lake, noting the perfect reflection of the early morning sky. Absentmindedly, he finally answered, "No, it was not."

Enoch started to ask him about it but decided that his son would tell him about it if he wanted to. Until then, he would leave it alone. "Well, we are awake now. Why don't we get an early start? Are you hungry?"

Methuselah stretched his arms and arched his back, "A little."

Enoch did the same and stood. "I think I'll go pick a few of those figs. They will make a nice breakfast for us." With that, he made his way toward the small grove. This gave Methuselah some time to collect his thoughts and get fully awake.

It wasn't long before they were on their way again. They found the road that led to Baalta and made their turn. A sense of foreboding permeated the silence and the familiar clip-clop of the horses' hooves. The men rode along that way for some time before seeing signs of farming, evidence that their destination was not far away. This only seemed to deepen the awful feeling. Neither man was looking forward to their arrival.

The roadway meandered left and right, up and down for a while, before leading upward toward the top of a ridge. Birds were singing their praises to the new day, and all sorts of creatures, great and small, foraging about along the picturesque country lane. Up and up they went until, finally, they crested the top of the ridge.

When the valley on the other side of the ridge fully presented itself, Enoch suddenly pulled back on the reins, bringing the carriage to a quick stop. Methuselah looked at his father, a bit bewildered by his actions, "Father, why did you stop? Is something wrong?" Enoch did not answer. Instead, Methuselah watched as his father slowly put down the reins and got out of the carriage, never taking his eyes off the valley before him. Methuselah followed suit and came around to where he found his father kneeling, blankly staring ahead.

"Father, what is the matter? What do you see?" Methuselah asked as he scanned the scene before him, desperate to find the source of his father's troubles.

Enoch's eyes gave away the fact that he was searching for an answer. After some time, he finally said something that did not seem to make sense to Methuselah, "A ghost from my childhood, I see a ghost from my childhood."

Methuselah narrowed his eyes and furrowed his brow. He again scanned the scene before him but only saw a quiet valley with a town and several small villages that lined a small river that wound its way through the valley. "I do not understand, Father. How do you see a ghost from your childhood?"

Enoch did not answer. His mind took him back to a dream—or a vision—he was not sure which, when he was fourteen. For, the valley before him now was the same one in that dream-vision. In the present, the air was still, and the sun was shining brightly over the hilltops. However, in his mind, he saw the darkened sky with the eerie red and green colors swirling and could feel the oddly chill winds that raced up the hill to where he now sat kneeling. He could feel the ground shaking beneath him and see the violent explosion of waters erupting upward into the atmosphere, punching a massive hole in the firmament above. He could hear, as if they were coming from somewhere in the past, or perhaps, somewhere in the future, the screams of people crying for mercy as they drowned in the torrential floods that quickly swallowed them. His heart raced anew as the memories of that terrible sight came rushing back.

Enoch was finally jostled back to the present as Methuselah shook him on the shoulders. "Father, what do you see?"

Finally, Enoch blinked and looked up at his son through the welling tears. He cleared his throat and swallowed hard, "My son, I have been here before. I have stood in this very place and seen the destruction of our world."

Methuselah was confused by the answer he had received, "What do you mean, Father? How are we standing here if this place has been destroyed?"

Enoch got slowly to his feet and wiped his eyes. He then looked at his son and shook his head, "Methuselah, what I mean is that I had a vision when I was a child. In that vision, I was standing in this exact spot." Enoch returned to the carriage, and Methuselah did the same as his father explained what he had seen so long ago. They did not travel from that spot for a long while as Enoch recited the story.

Methuselah listened intently until his father had finished. Then, after several moments of thoughtful silence, he asked, "Father, when will all this happen?"

Enoch only shook his head and snapped the reins to get the horses moving again. "I am not sure. I only know that it will not happen today." Deep inside, he knew exactly when it would happen. He looked at his son and recounted a different vision from thirty years before, wherein he was told what to name this son of his. In his mind, he said, "May you have a long life, my son."

———◊◊◊———

Simyaza had spent the night pacing to and fro across the floor of his den. He was not sure what he would do when his visitors arrived. He recited several options to himself but wanted to make the most of his opportunity. "Should I just have this man, Enoch, killed right away when he arrives, or should I welcome him, make him feel comfortable, and then kill him? When I kill him, should I have a henchman do it while I watch so I can laugh at him, or should I do it myself and add a personal touch? That would be nice, but that will not work. I cannot take a life. I will have to make someone else do it. I curse the Creator for limiting me this way!"

He went on for most of the night, talking to himself this way before his thoughts were finally interrupted by another presence in the room. He turned quickly to face a dark—even darker than he—figure hovering in the corner of the room. He dropped to one knee. "Master, I welcome you!"

The dark figure did not move from where it was. It only pulsated like wisps of black, sulfurous smoke caught in an oscillating draft, as if the blackness itself was breathing. When it finally spoke, it sounded like the voice was echoing back in on itself, yet it rattled Simyaza's teeth and pierced his ears as if it were inside his head. "Simyaza, I see that you are preparing for a visit. Do you know who it is that is coming to Baalta tomorrow?"

Simyaza dared not look directly at the darkness as he answered feebly, "I suspect that it is the man, Enoch, Master."

The figure flashed with a reddish tint at the sound of Enoch's name. "Yes. It is he, that accursed human, who dares to speak against me!" The voice rose to a disgusted crescendo as it spoke until Simyaza thought his ears would bleed if possible. It continued a bit calmer, "In fact, he and his son are already on their way."

Simyaza's curiosity was aroused, "He is coming here with his son? He must know that his life may be in danger. Why would he bring his son? Does he not know that I will have them both killed?"

The voice laughed insidiously at the thought, "You would enjoy that, wouldn't you, Simyaza?"

Simyaza smiled a bit, his thin lips twisting upward unnaturally, "Yes, Master. I would."

The voice resumed its earsplitting pitch again, "You will *not*! You will only do what I *tell* you to do! You are a worm, and you will not presume to do *anything* unless I tell you! Do I make myself clear?"

Simyaza's voice shook as he answered, "Yes, Master. Your will is mine."

The presence calmed again, "That is better. I can understand the thought of having them both killed. It *is* a pleasant thought. However, what I want is something far more pleasant to me. I do not care what happens to the boy, but I want his father to suffer. It would be too easy for him if he were just to die. Do you understand what I am saying, Simyaza?"

"Yes, I believe so," Simyaza answered.

The voice continued, "I want you to treat them with hospitality in the meantime. I have a plan. If it works the way I believe it will, the next few days will be very interesting. I am going now to plant an idea into the mind of Enoch's son. He is his first-born, you know."

Simyaza's countenance brightened at that news. "He is the first-born?"

The voice laughed again, "Yes. But, do nothing different until the time comes. Go on with the sacrifices as planned. If all goes my way, you will know what to do when the opportunity arises." With that, the presence made a quiet exit.

Simyaza waited until morning and summoned Telah. "Telah, find Ronin. Tell him to instruct the city gatekeepers that, when our two visitors arrive, they should allow them in without incident. They are to be escorted directly here and they are to be treated with every kindness. Do you understand?"

Telah's expression gave no sign of surprise. It never did. "Yes, Master. I understand. I will give him the message right away." He then turned and started to make his exit until Simyaza spoke again.

"Oh, and Telah, I want you to prepare our guests lodging for the night. I want them to be treated royally tonight. Have the cooks prepare a feast for them." Telah only nodded and continued out the door.

Chapter 17

AFTER A GIANT-SIZED BREAKFAST, GARDAN NOW stood next to Nahla, speaking softly into her ear. It had been a relatively quiet morning. The king and queen had spoken to him, asking him more questions about his childhood. They had not done it in a prying way but more to get to know him better, the way new friends would do. Gardan was now solemn, as he always was after bringing up those memories. However, he was not sad. It was more a feeling of gladness that the Lord had seen fit to bring him out of that darkness and into the goodness of the life he now enjoyed. These were the thoughts he was sharing with his huge friend now.

Nahla suddenly raised her head and eyed something behind him. When Gardan turned to look, he saw Analeah approaching slowly and cautiously, "Good morning, Gardan. Good morning, Nahla. I hope that I am not interrupting anything."

Gardan's heart swooned a bit at the sight of her. It was a strange and new sensation for him, and he was unsure what to make of it, "No. No, you are not interrupting anything at all. My friend and I were only telling each other stories from the past."

Analeah looked up at the two of them with an expression of awe. She still found it hard to comprehend the sheer size of the two giants. Yet, she also found the gentle, disarming nature of the two of them to be quite attractive. She liked them very much and could not help but smile at them, "These 'stories from the past' you are telling, are they stories of great adventure?"

Gardan thought momentarily and nodded, "In some ways, they are. They are more like stories of our redemption from lives of loneliness and sadness, and gratitude for our deliverance into lives of good friendships and worth, thanks to the Creator."

Analeah was taken aback by the pure honesty of his answer and the genuineness with which it was given. One word, however, captivated her, and she repeated it thoughtfully, "Redemption." She looked to the ground, sadness suddenly invading her countenance. "I wonder, Gardan. What does that feel like?"

Gardan was struck with compassion. He could see the pain on her face caused by the guilt of her past. He went down to one knee and gently spoke to her, "Dear lady, we have all fallen short of what we were created for. We have all made terrible mistakes in the past for which we think there could be no forgiveness. However, I have found that the Creator has a way of taking those mistakes and using them for our good. If only you ask, He can be trusted to forgive."

Analeah looked up at him, her eyes beginning to well, "How could anyone forgive me for what I have done?"

Gardan smiled gently, "Analeah, if little Asham did something wrong, something terrible, but asked your forgiveness in genuine sorrow for what he had done, would you not find compassion for him and forgive him?"

Analeah dabbed at her eyes and answered, "Yes, I suppose I would."

Gardan smiled broadly, "If you can forgive him, do you not think the One who created you, and knew from the beginning what you would do, could be even more forgiving than you?

Dear woman, I can see that you are infinitely sorry for what you have done. Trust me, the Lord knows it too. I suspect that He has already forgiven you. The question is if *you* can forgive *yourself*."

Analeah shook her head, "I do not think so. It hurts so much."

Gardan paused before speaking, "You know, when we make poor decisions, the Lord is good to forgive us for our sins. However, He is also our Father. In His infinite righteousness, He must use those poor decisions, and the pain they cause, to teach us not to make them again. In His forgiveness, there is no more condemnation, but there are still consequences. Those consequences are for our good. I suspect that you will always feel the pain of your decision. That pain can only heal over time. However, you must learn to accept that there is no more condemnation as far as the Lord is concerned. You have already been forgiven."

It was clear to Gardan that Analeah was struggling to understand what he was telling her. She only shook her head and spoke weakly, "I will have to think about what you said." With that, she turned and walked back into the house.

Gardan remained on one knee and closed his eyes. He spent some time after that in prayer, "Lord, please help her to feel Your love and forgiveness. And, Lord, I pray she will learn to forgive herself."

—⟨ೲೲ⟩—

As Enoch and Methuselah made their way down into the valley toward Baalta, they started noticing a few strange things. First, there was an absence of the usual songbirds that always accompanied any ride through the countryside. Second, and perhaps even more disturbing, the farms they passed by were either wholly overgrown with weeds and thistles or well-weeded but nearly dead.

"Father, what do you make of this?" Methuselah asked.

Enoch was as confused as his son, "I am not sure." Enoch stopped to look at the fields to the right of the road. The rows of wheat were perfectly manicured in even rows. The ground looked well watered, and there was no weed or thistle to be seen. However, the wheat was an unhealthy yellow, and the stalks were limp. What little grain could be seen on the wheat heads was grey and appeared to be moldy. Enoch shook his head and spurred the horses on.

Upon coming to the next field, their confusion deepened. Unlike the field before, this field was as green as any field could be. Still, the healthy grain that grew there was almost completely covered in even healthier weeds and thistles. As they slowly passed by, the men only shook their heads.

Methuselah never took his eyes off the spectacle, "Father, do you suppose that the farmer just abandoned his farm? It looks as if no one has worked the field in quite a while."

Enoch's attention was drawn to the little cottage just up the road, where he could see a man and a woman standing and staring out into the overgrown field. "I do not know, but perhaps these people could tell us."

When they reached the front of the house, Enoch pulled up on the reins bringing the carriage to a stop. "Hello," Enoch said with a smile.

The man and woman just looked at them for a moment. Their expression told Enoch that these people were not used to seeing strangers. But the apparent sadness in their faces also told him that they had much deeper worries than the two of them. "Hello, strangers," was all the man said.

Enoch and Methuselah exchanged glances before Enoch spoke again, "Is everything alright with you, Sir?"

The man gave him an odd look. "Is everything alright?" The man turned about with his hands out, gesturing toward his overgrown fields. "Does it look to you like everything is alright?"

Enoch could hear the strain in the man's voice and decided to proceed softly, "No. I can see that you have had some type of troubles. Is there anything we could do to help?"

The man looked almost insulted as he pointed to the rows of moist soil underneath the overgrowth. "Can you make dry ground moist again?" He now turned toward a small, empty ox stall on the side of his house. "Can you bring a dead ox back to life? If not, then I suppose you cannot help me."

Enoch and Methuselah were now fully confused by what the man had said. It was plain to see that the "dry" soil the man had pointed at was as black and healthily moist as any they had ever seen. And the "dead" ox he spoke of was not dead at all. In fact, it was, at that very moment, on the other side of the house, grazing on the healthy wheat in the unkempt field.

Enoch did not know how to respond, "I do not understand, Sir."

The man was now looking a bit confused himself. "What do you mean you do not understand? What is there to understand? My wheat is all dead from lack of water, and my ox has wasted away to nothing until it finally died this morning!" He looked to his wife, who, with tears streaming down her face, clutched onto a baby boy of about one year. "I am afraid we only have one choice now if we are going to save our farm." The man then collapsed down next to his wife and started crying with her.

Methuselah started to say something, but Enoch stopped him before he could. Enoch spoke, "I am sorry to have troubled you, Sir. We will not bother you anymore. Good day." With that, he spurred the horses on again. As they rode away, Methuselah gave his father a most inquisitive look. Once out of earshot of the strangers, Enoch said, "Methuselah, I know what you are thinking. I would be just as confused as you if not for what the Lord told me. It took me a while to catch on, but I finally realized why the man was acting so strangely."

Methuselah thought he might burst if his father did not tell him soon, "What, Father? What is making that man see things that are not there…or, at least, are not as they appear?"

"It is an illusion," Enoch said. "Simyaza has caused them to see things the way he wants them to see it. They have put their faith in Simyaza. The more they begin to trust in his lies, the more they begin to believe what he wants them to believe."

Methuselah was still confused, "I do not understand. Anyone can plainly see that his soil was good for growing, and that his ox was as fat and healthy as any. Why would he think he was dead?"

Enoch answered patiently, "Son, do you remember what Analeah told us about Simyaza? She said that the farms and businesses of those who refused to make the sacrifice would fail, but that the opposite would happen for those who did."

"Yes," Methuselah answered.

Enoch continued. "Well, what you just saw tells the story. Simyaza's power is not real. He only has illusions. The more the people believe his lies, the more powerful the illusion. Simyaza has told that man that he must sacrifice his son or his farm will fail. The man has begun to trust in what Simyaza told him so much that he has given himself over completely to the illusion of a failing farm. Where we can plainly see moist, fertile soil, he can only see dead, dry ground. Where we can see a healthy ox, he can only see a dead one. He believes so much in Simyaza's empty promises that, if he does give in and sacrifice his son, he will come back and see his ox alive and his fields green again."

Methuselah thought about it before speaking again, "But what about the other farms we saw? They were well kept and should have been healthy, but the wheat looked moldy and dying."

Enoch shook his head, "I suppose that, in those cases, the converse is true. The more they believe in Simyaza's blessings, the more the Lord will withhold *His* blessings. He cannot hon-

or their efforts if they insist on relying on the detestable sacrifices of their children for those blessings. They are reaping
their reward. However, as is often the case when men live in
such sin, my guess is that they believe the same delusion; that
everything is just fine. They probably see their crops as being
perfectly healthy."

The rest of the ride to Baalta was quiet as the two men
thought about what they had encountered. Enoch could see
that Methuselah was deeply disturbed but chose to let him
work it out in his own mind.

As they approached the city, they only gave each other a
look and took a deep breath to settle their nerves. Neither man
knew what to expect. However, they were surprised to get the
greeting they received when they reached the main city gate.

A large man armed with a menacingly large sword stepped
from the gatehouse to meet them, "Hello strangers. I take it
that you are Enoch. And, this must be your son, Methuselah."

Enoch was a bit shocked by the warm welcome, "Yes, we
are they."

The man smiled brightly, "Governor Simyaza is expecting
you. Welcome to Baalta." The man then turned and barked an
order to the gatekeeper, "Open the gate!" He turned back to
them, "If you would follow me, I will take you to Simyaza. He
is looking forward to meeting you both."

The two visitors exchanged a look that told the story. This
unexpected welcome did nothing to quell the uneasy feeling in
their stomachs.

Chapter 18

"**I** BELIEVE IT IS JUST WHAT THE POOR CHILD NEEDS," Adam said to the king, who was clearly disturbed by his request.

Eve now spoke up, "Yes, she needs this so badly. I think it would be a great blessing to her."

The king rubbed his face with both hands, "If I give my approval, would you at least reconsider taking a guard along with you? I would be worried about the two of you making such a journey alone."

Adam laughed as he answered, "My son, the two of us have managed to get along for over seven hundred years without any protection other than what the Creator has provided. I do not think that we will suddenly need it now."

The king looked over to his wife with a rather frustrated expression. The queen smiled as she spoke, "Seth, I believe it *would* be a great blessing to her. Besides, you are outnumbered. You know that you cannot win this argument."

He shook his head and threw his hands up in surrender, "Fine, go with my blessing. I am only the king. What say do I have in the matter?" He then stood, stepped down to where his parents stood, and embraced them lovingly. "Please, do be careful. The way of this world seems to be changing. It is not what it was seven hundred years ago. There are dark forces at work. I have recently been made all too familiar with that fact as of late."

His mother gently touched her son's face, "You are a good son to worry, but we will be alright. The Lord will protect us." With one final kiss, they turned and left the throne room.

—⁓—

Ednah and Naamah sat on the edge of the bed, smiling broadly at the sight and sound of the little one as he played. Asham cackled and laughed at Mirah as she pretended to make her doll dance up to him and kiss him. She would do it repeatedly, eliciting the same response every time. The two women almost simultaneously commented on how they missed that sound in their homes.

Julis was standing behind Tamari, brushing and arranging her hair in an attempt to decide how it would look for her wedding. Upon hearing the comments from the two women, she playfully turned and made a comment of her own, "You know, it will probably not be too long before you both have grandchildren to play with once Methuselah and Tamari are married."

Tamari suddenly shifted and turned to eye her little sister, pulling her hair out of Julis' hands, face fully in blush, "Julis!"

Naamah and Ednah could not help but laugh as Naamah lightly scolded her daughter, "Julis, do not tease your sister that way!" Then, with a playful glance toward Ednah, she continued, "Besides, given the way Jubal looks at you, your wedding, and perhaps, your own children, may not be too far off either."

It was now Julis who turned, hands on her hips and face in full blush. This brought a hearty laugh from Tamari. However, when the room full of women noticed that Jubal had been standing in the doorway and heard the whole thing, everyone was blushing. Jubal turned and quickly walked away, a bit embarrassed and wishing to be anywhere but there. Julis turned and gave her mother a scolding look of her own before running after him. The whole room soon erupted in laughter.

For a while afterward, the women would take turns giggling about the incident, which made everyone start laughing all over again. Analeah then came to the door, curious about it all, "What is so funny?"

Naamah answered vaguely, "Oh, just having some fun and embarrassing each other."

Analeah, who had been in a rather somber mood for most of the day, felt as if she was interrupting and decided to leave them to their fun. "Oh, I see. I do not want to interrupt. I was just checking on Asham. I'll just take him and go now. I am sorry if he has been any trouble."

She started toward him with her arms out to pick him up when Naamah spoke up, "Analeah, dear, I did not mean to make you feel as if you were interrupting. I am truly sorry if I did. And, I assure you, Asham has been no trouble at all. In fact, we were just saying how nice it was to hear the sound of a little one laughing again. We haven't heard that for a long time now."

Mirah spoke up now, "He has been so much fun to play with! He likes it when I do this." Mirah then danced the doll up to him and made it kiss him again. Asham cackled again, clapping his fat little hands together.

Analeah smiled at her, "I want to thank you for keeping him company and playing with him like this. I am afraid I haven't been in much of a playing mood lately."

Mirah looked at her with wide, honest eyes, "Oh, it's alright! He is much more fun than my dolls." All three women laughed.

Analeah's countenance almost at once became somber again. Ednah and Naamah noticed it and sensed that she needed to talk about something. Ednah glanced at Naamah, and Naamah understood what she meant. Naamah stood and addressed Mirah, "Asham looks like he could use a snack. Why don't we go and see if the cooks can find something for him?"

Mirah, who also liked the idea of a snack, jumped up with Asham in tow. "Alright, let's go." With that, they left Ednah and Analeah alone in the room.

Ednah gave it a moment before asking, "Is there something you want to talk about?"

Analeah sat on the bed next to her and took a deep breath, "I am so confused." She then flopped back on the bed and stared at the ceiling, "Gardan is very nice, isn't he?"

Ednah was a bit taken aback by the question. She suspected an attraction between the two of them but, for obvious reasons, brushed it aside. However, she now found herself in the position of having to discuss it directly. She said a silent prayer before answering the question. She responded cautiously, "Yes, Gardan is very nice. He has been a dear friend to our family for many years now."

Analeah continued to stare at the ceiling. "He is so different from anyone else I have ever met. I know he is a giant, but that isn't what I mean. It's just that I find him to be so genuine and honest." She now sat up and looked Ednah in the eye. "When he looks at me, it's as if he doesn't see what I have done in the past. He isn't judging me. He seems to genuinely care about me. It is as if he sees me for who I should be instead of who I am. Do you understand what I am saying? Does that make any sense?"

Ednah was unsure how to answer at first. Still, she found a gentle voice whispering in her ear and knew what to say, "Analeah, Gardan is an extraordinary soul. He has come from a past that most of us could not relate to. I believe it is in his nature to want to see the very best in the people he cares about, and we are all blessed to be a part of that small group of people. If he has chosen to call you a friend, you have a friend for life."

Ednah took a deep breath before saying more and hoped it would be taken well, "However, Analeah, I suspect that you have felt lonely for a very long time. I understand that you want someone that can fill that void in your life, but dear, you have to heal from your wounds. Right now, you feel as if you have lost everything that you knew in life. You have lost a child, a home, and friends you had when you were in Baalta. But you have to think about something else. I know you are angry and have been hurt by him, but you still have a husband."

Analeah's eyes widened as the anger inside started to surface, "He is *dead* to me! He is no husband! He forced me to sacrifice my son! What kind of husband is that? Oh, no; he is no husband! He is a *monster*!"

Ednah wanted to try and calm her down and put a gentle hand on her shoulder, "I know how you are feeling. I can understand…"

Analeah was having none of it, "You know how I am feeling? How could you possibly know how I am feeling? I have seen the way your husband looks at you. I see the way he treats you. I see the way Jaylon looks at Naamah. I see the way Methuselah looks at Tamari. I even see the way Jubal looks at Julis. You women are all loved so dearly by your men! It has been a long time, so long that I cannot even remember, since my, so-called, *husband* has looked at me that way!"

Analeah fell back on the bed again and sobbed deeply. "Can't you understand? I only want to be loved like you are. Is it so wrong for me to want to be loved by someone? Is it so wrong to want to feel love again?"

Ednah's eyes welled up with tears of compassion. "I do understand, Analeah. You want what has been taken from you. You want the life you had before Simyaza came to Baalta. You feel as though all your hopes and dreams have been stolen from you and replaced by the nightmare that you have been living.

There is absolutely nothing wrong with your wanting to be loved again. We all want to be loved and to feel love. But what you do not seem to realize is that you *are* loved."

Analeah huffed at that, "Oh, I suppose you are going to tell me that the Creator loves me. That seems to be all you people care about! Well, let me tell you something. It is *not* the same."

Ednah thought about it momentarily before answering, "You are right. It is not the same. It is better." Analeah huffed again, but Ednah continued, "You want the love of a man. I understand that, but you had that before and lost it. You want to love a man again, but you had *that* before and lost it."

Ednah took Analeah by the hand and pulled her upright so that she could now look her in the eyes. "Analeah, don't you understand? The love that the Creator can give you is a love that never goes away. No matter what you do, or have ever done, *nothing* can separate you from the love of God. It does not matter how you feel about Him. He is going to love you anyway. It is His nature to love us; all of us. All you need to do is accept and believe in that perfect love. It is the most wonderful gift He can give, and He gives it freely."

Analeah stared Ednah in the eyes. What Ednah was telling her did not make sense to her. She wanted to believe her, but her experiences in life had taught her differently. "No one gives love without wanting something in return, Ednah."

Ednah nodded, "That is what I am trying to explain to you. No man on earth, or woman for that matter, is capable of pure, unconditional love. You loved your husband at one time. But when he did what he did, you stopped loving him. Your love for him was conditional. When he did not treat you as you deserved to be treated, your love went away."

Analeah snapped back quickly, "Was I supposed to keep on loving him after what he did? Are you saying that I should have just ignored what he did and just go on like it never happened?"

Ednah shook her head, "Please, do not misunderstand what I am saying. It was a terrible thing that was done. I am not saying that you should have just excused it. I am only trying to make the point that love from one person to another is based on the condition of the treatment of one person to the other. If one person feels that the other is treating them wrongly, the love he or she feels for them can go away. However, when it comes to the Creator, He knows what we are capable of before we even do it. He knew what you and your husband were going to do long before it was done. Yet, even so, He loves you. He still wants to comfort you in your grief."

Analeah's eyes were welling up again, "What makes you think that I am being comforted? I am miserable! How is He showing me love when I feel the way I do?"

Ednah smiled gently and spoke softly, "Analeah, do you really think that we just happened to find you at that lake by coincidence? Do you really believe that we just happened to be going to the one person in the whole earth who could stop it from happening again?"

Ednah could see that what she was saying was beginning to strike a nerve with Analeah. She continued, "My dear, the Lord put you right where He wanted you. We have been blessed with the honor of showing you the love of the Creator. You say that what you did is so terrible that no one would ever care for you again if they knew about it. But we know about it, and we have done nothing but show you love and compassion. You have been with people who have accepted and embraced the perfect love of God; people who have also been guilty of doing terrible things in our past. However, we have been forgiven for those things. Do not misunderstand. We have had to live with the consequences of the poor decisions we have made but, by faith in Him and His free gift of grace, we are forgiven."

Analeah was starting to comprehend what Ednah was saying but still had doubts, "You people have been so nice to me, though. I do not see what you could have done so wrong that you would need His forgiveness. What have you done that was so bad?"

Ednah smiled again, "Analeah, we are all capable of evil. Perhaps it is something that no one else saw you do, or an evil thought about someone else. Maybe you told a lie to save yourself from punishment. We have all done these things and, on the surface, they may not seem too bad when compared to other sins, such as murder or stealing. However, to a perfect God, one sin is just as bad as another. He cannot abide by any sin, no matter how big or small."

Analeah was struck by that statement, "Then, how does anyone have a chance of pleasing Him?"

Ednah smiled broadly now, "That is where His gift of grace comes in. All He asks is that we acknowledge Him as the Creator and trust Him with our lives. He wants nothing more than our faith."

Analeah was thinking deeply now, "But, do I *then* have to live a sinless life to keep His love? Who can do that?"

Ednah answered happily, "No, Analeah. You do not have to live a sinless life to keep His love. Remember, I told you that He would never stop loving you. He knows that we can never be perfect. He does not expect us to be perfect. He only asks that we trust in His perfection and His grace to cover our sins. That does not mean that we can go out and live any way we want and still expect Him to forgive us. But, if we truly appreciate the gift He has given, we will *want* to live our lives in a way that is pleasing to Him. Do you understand what I am trying to say?"

Analeah's eyes were welling up again, but this time, they were tears of a different kind. "Tell me, Ednah, what must I do to receive that gift of grace? I think I could use some grace in my life right now."

Ednah's eyes were moistening as she asked a simple question, "Analeah, the gift is free for the asking. Do you want His forgiveness?" Analeah only nodded. "Then, all you need to do is ask Him."

Analeah's heart was broken. A torrential flood of sobs and repentant tears came gushing out as she cried out to God for His forgiveness and His grace. Ednah gently patted her on the leg and quietly slipped out of the room. Analeah had some personal business with the Creator, and she wanted to give them the space to do it.

Chapter 19

*E*NOCH AND METHUSELAH HAD FOLLOWED THE gate guard through the dusty and somewhat strange streets of Baalta. What they found strange were not the streets themselves, although they were unusually dry. It was the people. Many of them were thin and sickly-looking. They were grey in color with eyes sunken back as if they were starving. Yet, they acted as if they were perfectly content. On the other hand, other people looked healthy and well-fed but acted as if they were sad and hopeless.

When their carriage passed through the open market, Enoch and Methuselah were nearly overwhelmed by the smell of rotting fruit. They watched as the frail-looking customers bartered with the equally frail-looking sellers for what appeared to be molded loaves of bread and rancid produce. When one particular woman arrived at the desired cost of a rather soft and yellow melon, she cackled as if she had made the deal of the day, obviously ecstatic about the purchase. It would have been a very odd scene any other time, but given what they had discovered on their way through the valley, everything seemed to fit the scenario.

Upon arriving at what appeared to be the largest residence in the city, Enoch and Methuselah were led inside, where a tall, thin, very dark figure of a man met them with a sinister smile and a rather uncomfortable welcome, "Hello, Enoch! It is an honor to have you here." He then turned his attention to Methuselah, "And this must be your son, Methuselah. Welcome! I am Simyaza, the governor of Baalta. Please, come sit and make yourselves comfortable." Simyaza pointed toward a well-cushioned couch situated directly across from an oversized, elaborately carved chair where he seated himself. "We have much to discuss, do we not?"

Father and son exchanged a glance and tentatively sat on the couch. After an awkward silence, Enoch spoke, "Thank you, Simyaza. Yes, I believe we do have some things to discuss." He cleared his throat and asked the question that had been on his mind since they arrived: "I am curious, Simyaza. How did you know we were coming, and how did you know who we were? It was my belief that we were coming unannounced."

Simyaza waved off the question as if it were nothing, "Oh, I suppose it is part of my nature to know everything that happens in my little valley. Besides, I believe you have already met one of my people. He told me that he thought someone may be coming to see me. It was easy, due to the circumstances, to deduce who it may be."

Enoch was a bit surprised by the answer, given that Jeru was not told anything about the visit, but decided to let that go, "I see. Well, speaking of Jeru…"

Simyaza put up a hand to stop Enoch from speaking and feigned humility, "Please, let me apologize for Jeru's incompetence. As is often the case with the people you employ, he completely misunderstood his mission to the Royal City. If only he had properly followed my instructions, I believe his visit would have gone much better for him. You see, when he returned to Baalta, he told me what happened. I must tell you; I am embarrassed by his misrepresentation of me."

Then, as if he had suddenly remembered something, he asked, "Oh, where are my manners? You are probably thirsty after your journey. Would you like something to drink while we talk?"

Methuselah held up a hand as if to say "no." Enoch, wanting to appear at ease, although he was not, answered, "Yes, please. That would be nice."

Simyaza smiled widely. Enoch noted that smiling was something that Simyaza was not good at. It appeared as though he had not had much practice at it. Simyaza then called toward the door, "Telah!" The sickly-looking servant came to the doorway without a word. Simyaza barked his order, "Bring some wine for our guests." Telah only nodded and disappeared.

Simyaza then returned to the conversation seamlessly, "As I was saying, I was rather embarrassed by Jeru's behavior while in the Royal City. I assure you; he was severely punished for it. You see, I was only concerned for the welfare of the young lady and her child. As you can imagine, when they came up missing without a word, her husband was quite worried. This kind of thing does not happen here in Baalta. Naturally, I could not just ignore one of my citizens' concerns. Her husband, Jotham, has been a good and loyal citizen of Baalta. When he came to me with his problem, I had no choice but to help."

Simyaza now stood and paced around the room in order to add some animation to his speech, "You see, I do not see my people here as mere citizens. They are like…my children. When one of them are missing or in some trouble, it is my duty to see to it that my citizen gets back to safety. However, it is my understanding that Jeru went to the king and demanded her return. That was obviously not the way to handle the situation. That was also not his job. His job was merely to find out where she had gone and see that she was safe. She apparently was. At that point, all he needed to do was report back to me. Then, all this ugly business could have been avoided."

At that moment, Telah returned carrying a tray with a jug of wine and three goblets. He sat the tray down and poured the wine into each of them. He then served Simyaza first to let the guests know where they stood. After that, he served Enoch and Methuselah. Methuselah did not really want the wine but, being a bit nervous and needing something to do with his hands, picked up the goblet and held it in his lap. Simyaza watched and waited for Enoch to do the same, in so doing, signaling for him to try it. Enoch picked up on this and decided to take a sip as protocol suggested. Upon putting the goblet to his lips, he was almost overcome by the odor of spoiled grapes. He quickly decided to only act as if he were taking a sip. It was all he could do not to make a face. He then slowly put the goblet on the table in front of him.

Methuselah, however, was not as cautious. He quickly took a full sip. His face contorted, and he immediately spat the wine back into the goblet. Simyaza narrowed his eyes at him and acted as if he had been slighted, "Is there something wrong with the wine?"

Enoch quickly spoke up in order to keep the meeting calm, "Oh, you must excuse him. You see, we are not used to drinking strong wine. He is just not used to fermented drinks."

Simyaza sat back in his chair and slowly relaxed, seemingly satisfied with Enoch's explanation, "I see."

Enoch let the moment pass, taking another fake sip of his wine before speaking again, "Well, Simyaza, what you said is all well and good, but Jeru commented that you did not 'allow' people to leave Baalta. What did he mean by that?"

Simyaza put his goblet on the table and sat back silently, making a steeple with his long boney fingers as he thought about the question, "As I said before, I see the people of Baalta as my children. If one of your children, like Methuselah here, were to run off and leave you with no explanation, would not you be upset by that? I dare say that you would react much the same as I. Your concern would be for his safety. You would want him to come back home where you can protect him. I suppose, if it is such, my only crime is in being too protective over my citizens." Simyaza, apparently very satisfied by his cunning answer, grinned widely.

Enoch, however, was not so satisfied, "I understand what you are saying. But Analeah seemed absolutely terrified by the prospect of coming back to Baalta. She believes that there is another reason that people are not allowed to leave the city. Do you have any idea what that reason might be?" Enoch did not want to tip his hand that he knew about the sacrifices; he was hoping to bait Simyaza into an admission.

Simyaza narrowed his eyes at him. His tone became less than friendly, "Listen. If her husband treated her roughly, perhaps that is why she ran away. It may be that her husband is weak and stupid, as Jeru suggests. She may have left to try and find a better man. Whatever her reason for doing what she did, I cannot say." Simyaza now stood and began pacing around the room again, his voice becoming a bit more menacing, "I will say this, however. This city, and the valley surrounding it, is my jurisdiction. How I run things here is not for anyone else to say! I do not care what you, your son, or King Seth thinks of me or my methods! So, if you have an accusation to make, I suggest you make it now."

Enoch could see that things were quickly getting out of hand and decided to try and defuse the situation, "Please, Simyaza, we are here in peace. If my question made you think otherwise, I am sorry. We came here alone. We brought no army and no ill intent. My son and I are only an informal delegation. The king was told some disturbing things. We are only here to ask questions. If you are uncomfortable, perhaps we should try again later when things calm down."

Simyaza stared at him for a moment. He remembered what his master told him and decided to take Enoch's advice. He quickly resumed his more jovial demeanor, "Of course, you are right. It is just that, where my little valley is concerned, I can be a bit overprotective. It is almost time for dinner. Let's resume our discussion after a good meal."

Enoch agreed, "That sounds like a good idea. In the meantime, my son and I should probably find a place to spend the night."

Simyaza acted hurt, "Please, my friends. You will stay here in my home. I have plenty of room. You are my honored guests." With that, he again called for his servant, "Telah, show our guests to their room. See that they are comfortable and let them know how long it will be before dinner."

Telah silently nodded and stood sideways at the door while holding out a hand toward the other room. In doing so, he signaled to the guests that they should follow his directions. Enoch and Methuselah got up and exited the room. After passing through the doorway, they waited for their guide to lead the way. Telah, without even glancing at them, passed by, led them down a hallway, and stopped at an open door. Again, he held out a hand to signal that they should enter the room. They did so. Once inside the room and before they could turn to look at Telah, the door was unceremoniously closed behind them, leaving the two men alone.

Enoch and Methuselah exchanged wide-eyed expressions. Enoch spoke with a slight chuckle, "I guess this is our room."

Methuselah smirked back toward the door, "I suppose it is."

The two men then scanned their surroundings. The room was furnished simply. There were two small beds in the two far corners of the room with a humble little table between them upon which sat a single oil lamp. The beds were adorned with a simple, uncovered pillow and a light blanket. The walls were completely bare, and the room had no window openings. It looked as if the room had not been used in a very long time, and it was obvious that any visitors were not to get too comfortable.

Enoch offered a single observation, "It is a far cry from the king's residence, but it will serve the purpose."

Methuselah only shrugged his shoulders, his mind on other things. "Father, that wine was spoiled. I don't know how you could drink it without even making a face. How did you do that?"

Enoch chuckled again, "Oh, yes. The wine was quite spoiled. But I did not drink it. As soon as I put it to my lips, I could tell it was spoiled. I only pretended to take a few sips. I assure you; it was still hard not to make a face."

Methuselah returned the chuckle, "I saw you take a sip and didn't think twice about it until I had already taken it in. It was disgusting!"

Enoch laughed again, "I suppose if you are still thirsty I can have Telah bring you more."

Methuselah smirked. "No, thank you. I believe I have had enough." The men exchanged another laugh before Methuselah asked a pertinent question that naturally followed, "If the wine is spoiled and everything is backward from normal, what might our dinner taste like tonight?"

Enoch thought about it, "You know, that is a good question." Enoch sat on the bed and watched as dust billowed into the air. "I suppose we should just expect that all the food we will be served is going to be spoiled. We obviously cannot eat spoiled food, but we must be careful not to offend Simyaza any more than we already have. We will have to be cunning."

Methuselah was taken aback by his father's comment, "Why do we have to be careful not to offend *him*? Given what he is, I would think *his* feelings do not matter."

Enoch held up a hand, "I understand what you are saying, but we must remember that we are here on a peaceful mission. If it comes to war, we do not want it to be due to a lack of diplomacy on *our* part. We just need to get what answers we can and report them back to the king. As far as dinner is concerned, it would probably be a good idea to get to our own provisions from our carriage and bring them in. That way, no matter what happens, we will still be able to eat a good meal."

Methuselah agreed, "Perhaps we could tell them that we want to take a walk around the city before we eat."

Enoch smiled, "Good idea. Let's go."

Chapter 20

THE KING HAD BEEN ASKED A DIRECT QUESTION but did not want to answer, "Where are my mother and father? Well…they…had an errand to run. Is anything the matter? Perhaps I could help you."

Analeah could tell that the king was being evasive in his answer but assumed he had a good reason. "No. I just wanted to tell your mother something. That's all. Do you know when they will be back?"

The king could truthfully answer this question without any qualms, "I do not know exactly. They should be back within a few days anyway."

Analeah was a bit disappointed with the answer. She was hoping to tell Mother Eve about her very recent experience with the Creator. She felt as if she would burst if she did not tell someone. She had been so depressed for so long, but now her heart felt light. She had carried her burden for what felt like an eternity, but she was now free of it. She was able to leave it at the throne of God and walk away carrying only joy and gratitude. She felt clean, blessedly clean.

The king could see that she was disappointed. However, he could also see something different about her. Even through her disappointment, he could see what looked like contentment. "I am sorry that Mother is not here for you right now, but Janis is here. Would you like to speak with her? You have the look of a woman who might explode if she doesn't tell someone something. Am I right?"

Analeah could not help but smile and blush, "I am free, My King! I am free!"

The king was a little surprised at the sudden show of positive emotion from the woman who had looked so downtrodden since she had arrived. He could not help but smile along with her. "What do you mean, Child?"

Analeah said again, "I am free! I asked the Creator for His forgiveness, and He granted it! He has taken all my shame and guilt and thrown it into the sea. I feel so light and free!"

The king stood to his feet and threw his hands in the air, "That *is* wonderful news!" He then went to the door at the rear of the platform and yelled into it, "Janis! Janis, can you hear me?" He obviously heard an answer and yelled again, "Come out here! I have exciting news." He walked back over to face Analeah and rubbed his hands together in front of him like a child who was about to get a sweet treat.

The queen then entered through the doorway, looking a bit puzzled at the two smiling faces that greeted her. "What is all the excitement about? What has happened?"

The king motioned for Analeah to tell her the good news. Analeah did so, "My Queen, I am free! The Creator has forgiven me my sins and I am free! My soul feels clean for the first time ever and I had to tell someone!"

The queen smiled broadly and stepped down to embrace her. "That is wonderful, Analeah. I can see your happiness all over you."

Analeah now had tears of joy in her eyes, "Thank you, My Queen. Thank you for allowing me to tell you. I wanted to tell someone, but I couldn't find anyone until I came in here and found the king."

Queen Janis looked at her wide-eyed, "You mean that we are the first to be told?"

Analeah nodded her head, "Yes."

The king threw his hands in the air again, "Praise God!" He then looked as if he had just had a thought, "We *must* have a celebration for you! We will have music and dancing and lots of good food. We will have it in the courtyard and invite the entire Royal City to celebrate with us."

Analeah was not prepared for that, "But, My King, it is true that I am very happy. However, I do not think that the entire city would find it so exciting as all that."

The king looked at her with all seriousness, "Analeah, there is something that you must understand. When one is lost, but then is found, it is cause for celebration. The Royal City is a big family. When you entered the city, you became a part of this family. If a family member or a child is lost, it grieves the whole family. But when that child has found her way home, the whole family celebrates. You have spent so much time thinking of yourself as worthless, but that does not mean that it was true. No matter what you thought of yourself, you were never worthless. You—*just you*—are worth throwing a party over. There is also something else you should realize. Yes, we are celebrating your homecoming. However, we ultimately have to celebrate the One who has brought you home. All the glory goes to Him. For, without His grace, none of us would have anything to celebrate."

Analeah was overwhelmed. She fell into the waiting arms of the queen and cried the humble tears of a woman of newfound worth.

—◦◦◦—

Jaylon had spent most of the day exploring the city with his two servants, Edgar and Targus. He had decided to leave the women to their wedding plans. He was not one for that sort of thing. Besides, since his recent conversation with Father Adam, he wanted to try and get to know his two most trusted servants better. As it turned out, he was surprised at how much he did not know about them.

Edgar had worked for him for nearly twelve years now. He oversaw all of Jaylon's household affairs. He had proven himself loyal and trustworthy in all aspects of his duties. However, after all those years of service, Jaylon found that he could not even name Edgar's wife and son. His wife, Alleah, was Naamah's seamstress and had come to work for them ten years before. It was there that the two of them had met. His son, Oden, was born to them four years ago.

The three men sat under a tent in the city's market, drinking mugs of fruit juice as Edgar shared his story, "Oh, by the way, Sir, I do not believe I ever properly thanked you for the gift of that beautiful blanket your wife gave us for my son when he was born. My wife and I were greatly appreciative."

Jaylon was ashamed to say that he was not even aware that Edgar was married or had a son, much less that they had received a gift from his household. In his shame, he simply replied, "You are welcome, Edgar."

Jaylon now turned to Targus. He knew that Targus had worked for him for a while but could not say how long exactly. He also knew that Targus was second in command of his mining operations and had also proven to be a valued employee. Sadly, that was all Jaylon could recall. Jaylon tried to hide this by asking the vague question, "Targus, how about you? How are you finding things these days?"

Targus did not know precisely what the question meant but was aware that Jaylon seemed a bit uneasy and decided to talk about the only thing he had ever really discussed with him, "Things at the mine are going well. We are finishing up excavating the original mine and starting work at the second location at the far end of the valley. It appears to be promising. We have already found some very nice emeralds and even a ruby or two. They are small, but who knows but that there may be some larger ones in there somewhere."

Jaylon was indeed put at ease a bit by Targus' answer, "That is wonderful! I had not heard about the rubies. I have been so busy with this wedding and all that it entails that I'm afraid I have not been fully engaged in the mines as usual."

Targus held up a hand of understanding, "That is fully alright, Sir. When my daughter was married last year, it was all I could do to keep my mind straight too. It is good that you have a wife who can keep track of all those things for you. I wish I had that benefit when my daughter was married. It was hard on me to do it all by myself."

Jaylon was dumbfounded by Targus' statement. Before now, he would not have been able to say if Targus was even married. Now, he found that he had a daughter who had married last year and that he was apparently a widower. In his humility and shame of not knowing either, he decided to own up to it and ask a few hard questions, "Please forgive me, Targus, but I was not aware that your daughter was married last year. I was also not aware that you were raising her alone. What happened to your wife?"

Targus took a deep breath as he began to fidget with his mug, staring at it, but obviously not thinking about the mug at all, "Well, I was married to my sweet Dahlia for fifteen years before she became pregnant with Sonee, my daughter. Before that, we were not even sure that Dahlia could have any children. We were so happy to find out that she was with child. We made all these wonderful plans. Back then, we lived in a small house in a little village in the south of Nod. I built another room on to the house and Dahlia decorated it so nicely. I even built a little bed for Sonee."

Targus continued to stare at his mug with a smile of remembrance. However, he took another deep breath to brace himself and solemnly continued, the smile disappearing, "When the time for Sonee to be born was still a long time away, it became apparent that something was wrong. Dahlia became more and more weak and sickly. We called for the midwife to look at her. She said that, if Dahlia continued to carry the child, she would probably die. The midwife said that the only way to save my wife was to take the child. I was heartbroken. I told the midwife to do whatever she had to do, but save my wife."

Jaylon was now feeling some of the evident emotions on his servant's face. However, he was now feeling for him as a friend and not an employer. He instinctively put a hand on his shoulder.

Targus wiped a tear away from his eye as he continued, "But Dahlia would have none of it. She scolded me, 'I will not let her take my child! If I have to die to give my child life, so be it!' I tried to argue with her, but she was a strong-willed woman. Ultimately, I could only pray to the Lord that both would live. However, as the day approached, Dahlia became worse until her water broke. When that happened, she just looked at me and smiled. She said, 'Take care of our child. Tell her I love her every day.' Then she died.

"The midwife pushed me out of the room and went to work. A little while later, she brought me Sonee. She put her in my arms and said, 'Here is your little girl.' I said, 'My little girl? How did Dahlia know it was going to be a girl?' The midwife only shrugged her shoulders but, after some time, I came to see that the Lord was giving me a sign of His love. He was showing me that, although my wife was not going to see my daughter grow up, He had given her a glimpse of her future to comfort her. My wife loved the Lord, and the Lord was showing me that He loved her too. In that, I can at least be sure that one day, when our time on this earth is complete, my daughter and I will see Dahlia again."

All three men were now wiping tears from their eyes. A few days before, Jaylon thought he knew all he needed to know about his two most-trusted servants. However, now he felt as though he had come to know a few intimate details about his two new friends. He now knew that Father Adam was right, and he would be forever richer for it.

Chapter 21

AS ENOCH AND METHUSELAH WERE MAKING THEIR way out of the house, they were met by Simyaza, waiting at the door as if he were expecting them. "You look to be going somewhere. I would be delighted if I could join you. I would like to show you around my little city. There are a few things I would like you to see."

The two men exchanged a glance before Enoch answered him, "Well, we were just going to get a few things from our carriage and perhaps take a walk outside to get our appetites going."

Simyaza gave them one of his uncomfortable smiles, "That is fine. I will have what you need brought in for you. In the meantime, we could walk together."

Enoch clearly had no choice, "Do not trouble anyone with our things. Let's take that walk. We will just get what we need on our way back in afterward." Simyaza smiled and nodded as he opened the door and led them out.

The sun was soon going to make its descent behind the low mountains beyond the small city. It gave off a strange yellow illumination against the dirty walls of the meager homes that lined the dusty streets. In most cities, the people would have been busy and bustling to and fro down the thoroughfares, packing up their wares and carting them home for the day. However, Baalta was not most cities. Although a few of the city's merchants were doing just that, they didn't seem to have much purpose in their gates. They seemed aimless; empty; vapid; utterly devoid of hope, and lost in their mundane existences.

As the three men strolled by, people would nod and smile at Simyaza and his guests. But it seemed to Enoch that they were acting more out of fear than friendliness, more reservation than respect. Enoch also noticed that, upon seeing Simyaza, the women would turn away or disappear into their homes. In the instant that they looked at him, there was no respect. Hatred was in their eyes, a clear look of disdain. If the man of the house were around, they would bow deeply to the ground in a show of respect, but their eyes showed a hint of the same kind of contempt.

Simyaza nodded back to them as he spoke to Enoch and Methuselah, "You see? The people of Baalta have the deepest respect for me. They know that they can trust me to take good care of them. When I first came here, they were without direction; each man only caring about his own tiny part of the city. He would take care of his little family, but seemingly show no regard for his neighbor. They were only interested in themselves, and what *they* needed."

At this point, Simyaza stopped and faced his guests directly, "But, since I've been here, I have been trying to instill in them a sense of…community. I have taught them that one man and his family is not the only thing that is important. I have taught them that their neighbor's wellbeing should be just as important as their own. Do you not believe that you are somewhat responsible for your neighbor's wellbeing, Enoch?"

Enoch thought momentarily about the question, "Yes, in a way, I do believe that we should look out for each other."

Simyaza smiled and turned to continue their walk. "You see, we are not so different. That is what I am trying to instill in them. However, I have found that this sense of community is not always enough without the proper leadership to oversee things, to make things run smoothly in a direction that benefits everyone. And, as that goes, I have also found that the people must have the proper respect for that leadership. As I said before, these people are my children. I cannot have the respect of all my children if one of them refuses to recognize me as their leader; even their father, if you will. So, in an effort to convince them all, I have had to make an example of a few."

Methuselah's curiosity was whetted by his last statement, "An 'example?' How do you mean. In what way do you do that?"

Simyaza furrowed his brow in a show of concern, "I must tell you, it is the part of my responsibility that I least enjoy. But, you see, that is where the sense of community comes into play. It is not me, per say, that has to do this. It is their own neighbors who act for the betterment of everyone. I allow *them* to put pressure on the one who needs correction. In this way, they can more easily recognize that they are acting outside the norm. They can then see that, if all their neighbors feel that they are doing something wrong, then it is most likely themselves who are the problem. This way they can see that they are no more important than anyone else. They are all the same and should all be working ultimately toward the same goal, the betterment of the entire community."

As they continued walking, Enoch was deep in thought about the discussion. He did, however, notice that an odor was getting stronger and stronger as they walked along. He pushed this out of his mind and focused on the conversation at hand. He could see that Simyaza was well-versed in his deception. If one did not know any better, one could be easily drawn in by his logic.

He decided not to challenge Simyaza directly but to change the course of it instead, "What about matters of faith? Where do you stand on that?"

Simyaza straightened his back and seemed to growl a bit, "Ah, faith. That has been a most difficult problem to overcome. By its very nature, faith is different from one man to another. One man can staunchly believe in one thing while another man believes just as heartily in another. This, of course, ultimately causes strife within a community. I believe that the only way a community can truly come together is if they all put their faith in the same thing. In this way, a point of contention—I think the *biggest* point of contention there is—is fully eliminated from the equation."

Enoch was now getting to the crux of their entire mission. He wanted to follow up on the point, but the odor invading his senses was becoming so strong that it could no longer be ignored, "I must ask you, what is that stench? It has been getting stronger and stronger the longer we walk."

At that moment, the men rounded a corner, and Simyaza raised an open hand toward the epicenter of the nauseating smell, "This is the answer to your question about the odor *and* the problem of faith."

Enoch and Methuselah were both stopped where they were, sick in their stomachs and in their hearts at the sight. There before them was the city's furnace. It was in the center of a large, open square that was big enough for the entire populace of Baalta to fit within. It seemed empty now as Enoch and Methuselah scanned the area…almost empty.

One woman was leaning against a wall, blankly staring at the monstrosity in the center of the square. She was young and pretty. She was also clearly expecting a child very soon. She just stood there with tears in her eyes as she lovingly rubbed her protruding belly. When she finally noticed the three men watching her, she stood straight up and walked down the wall and around the corner out of sight.

Simyaza, silently but derisively, watched her disappear. The scornful expression then left his face, and he turned his attention back to the furnace. It was easy to see that he was not repulsed in the least by the abomination that stood before him. He seemed to look at it with some measure of delight as if it were his favorite place to be.

Enoch could see the pride in Simyaza's eyes. He could even see a faint smile on his face, a wicked smile that somehow looked much more natural than the smiles he had worn for them before. Enoch decided to try and keep his head, although, within his spirit, he was seething. He knew full well what Simyaza used the furnace for but wanted to have him admit it directly, "I do not understand what you mean exactly, Simyaza. How does the city's furnace solve the 'problem of faith,' as you put it?"

Simyaza was not fooled in the least by Enoch's coyness. He turned and stared him directly in the eyes for a few awkward moments, feeling him out and trying to see if he would blink. Enoch did not. He only returned the stare until it was Simyaza who could not withstand the little contest any longer and spoke, "Enoch, I am not a mere man. I think you already know that, so I will not insult your intelligence by trying to hide that fact. I have been given certain…powers over this valley. I believe that you must have noticed on your way into the valley that some of the farms were healthier than others, did you not?"

Enoch answered simply, "Yes, I noticed that."

Simyaza continued, "It is my doing. I have in my hands the power of life and death. I can cause a farm to flourish, or I can cause it to wither and die." Simyaza waited to see if Enoch was impressed by this but saw that his expression had never changed. Enoch seemed to be completely nonplussed by Simyaza's claims of power. It was all Simyaza could do not to lose his temper at Enoch's lack of respect. Still, he pushed it back and continued, "Anyway, it is my desire to give my blessings to all the children of Baalta and to make their farms and businesses flourish. I truly do desire that. However, to ensure everyone's faith is pointed in one direction, I had to institute a…system, if you will, that would accomplish this; a system of sacrifice."

Enoch was beginning to be genuinely sickened by the utterly callous way in which Simyaza spoke about the Lord's people but continued to suppress his true feelings. He only said one word in order to prod Simyaza into saying more. It was all he felt he could get out before letting his true emotions show, "Sacrifice?"

Simyaza now faced the two men directly, "You see, if I just blessed everyone equally without requiring something in return, some of them would just attribute their prosperity to whatever god they chose to believe in. Then we would still have the problem of faith to contend with. However, if I require something from them in order that they receive my blessings, it helps them to understand that their faith needs to be in me. It makes no sense for them to put their faith in a god that they cannot even see. My system of sacrifice enables them to believe in something tangible; to believe in some*one* tangible. To feel like they have a chance to please the one that they have placed their faith in."

Simyaza waited to speak again. He wanted to watch the men and see their reactions to what he was saying, but again, he seemed to be getting little. "I know the young lady you took to the Royal City told you what that sacrifice entails. I can understand that it must seem rather…extreme to your sensibilities. But you must understand, the sacrifice must be great in order to engender the strength of faith that is required to keep a community working together for a single purpose. The sacrifice must be one of great value to the person. Otherwise, they would see my blessings as being of little value. Do you understand what I am saying? This way, when they sacrifice something as precious to them as a child, they will be able to justify it in their minds by attributing that same importance to the blessing. And, as a reward for their great faith and trust in me, I bless them richly with the promise of success and happiness. A reward that any of my children will tell you is well worth the sacrifice. I give them *life*."

At this point, Enoch's blood was boiling in his veins. He looked over and saw the same anger evident on Methuselah's face. He saw that Methuselah's mouth was open but heard no sound. He thought he was left speechless at the sheer audacity of their host. Enoch, however, had had enough. He turned back to Simyaza and was fully prepared to let his righteous rage loose upon the demonic angel of Lucifer. He opened his mouth but found he was struck dumb. He tried again and again but could not speak.

He just stood there, looking into the face of evil, but could not say a word. Simyaza had a look of confusion on his face as he stared back. Enoch felt as if his tongue were suddenly made of wood. He finally decided to close his eyes to calm himself down. He then said a little prayer in his mind, "Lord, help me! Give me your voice."

At that moment, he heard a small voice in his ears that sounded like a gentle stream washing over smooth pebbles, "Enoch, open your mouth and speak the words I give you. It is not yet time for anger."

Enoch opened his eyes again and opened his mouth. The words that came forth were not his own, for he could not imagine saying the words that came out. "Simyaza, my son and I cannot stay at your house tonight. You have given us much to think and pray about. We will camp outside the city and come back in the morning. We will be present at the sacrifice that you have planned for tomorrow."

Simyaza was now fully confused, "The sacrifice planned for tomorrow? How did you know about that? I do not recall telling you about that yet."

Enoch did not answer the question. He only grabbed his son by the arm and began walking back toward Simyaza's house, "We will be back in the morning."

Simyaza stood silently and watched them walk away. When they disappeared around the corner, he turned his attention back to the furnace. "You and your son will be more than *present* for the sacrifice tomorrow." The evil smile returned as he quietly, gleefully laughed to himself.

Chapter 22

*I*T WAS EARLY MORNING AT THE KING'S RESIDENCE, and the sun had only begun to lightly show the evidence of its rising upon the misty horizon. Gardan was wide awake. He had tried to go back to sleep, but something within his soul would not allow it. Nahla was also awake, seemingly troubled by something herself. Gardan sat against a large tree and absentmindedly rubbed her head, "You too, girl?" Nahla grumbled deep within her belly in an affirmative answer. He sat and thought for a while, but the only thing he could think was one word; pray. "I do not even know what I am supposed to pray for," Gardan thought. However, he finally gave in and began to do so.

Just about the time he started, he heard a door close and looked toward the house. There he saw Jaylon walking his way. He asked, "Jaylon, were you having trouble sleeping too?"

Jaylon rubbed his eyes and shook his head, "Yes, I suppose I was. I do not understand it, but I sense that the Lord wants me to pray. I started to do that, but felt pressed to come out here with you."

Gardan looked at him and shook his head, "Well, I guess we should just…" At that moment, they both heard the same door open and could see the figures of the king and queen approaching. Behind them were Ednah, Naamah, Tamari, and

Julis. As Julis turned to close the door, she stopped because Jubal, Targus, and Edgar were coming out too. Behind them were Mirah and Analeah, with little Asham in tow.

They all gathered under the huge tree surrounding Gardan and turned to watch the procession of people coming out of the doorway. Many of the king's servants came out as well. The door finally shut, and everyone looked at each other with smiles and laughed. It was then that others began to appear. They seemed to come from every corner of the city, all with the same bewildered look on their faces.

The king greeted them as they filed in around the tree. Finally, when it looked as if everyone who was coming had arrived, the king stood atop a table and shouted, "Dear friends, it appears that we have all been visited by the Spirit of the Creator this morning for a great purpose; to pray. I do not, and I suspect that many of you do not know exactly what we are praying for. However, we will pray as the Spirit leads us." With that, the king began to pray. Some prayed quietly amongst themselves, while others prayed aloud. A few people even sang songs of praise. Altogether, it was a beautiful scene as the sound of God's people crying out to Him rose like a sweet aroma to the Lord. A tangible feeling of joy and peace filled every heart in the assembly.

"… and I commit him into Your hands." Enoch awoke startled by the sound of his own voice. It took him a few moments to realize that he had been praying in his sleep. He looked over at Methuselah and could see that his lips were moving rapidly and his arms were raised in praise, but he, too, was still sleeping.

Enoch looked around to scan the horizon. They had made camp the night before just outside the city gates and spent much of the evening discussing and praying about what was to come. When they first arrived, they both had a heavy despair that seemed to oppress them, but now Enoch felt at peace. He thought about the last line of his prayer that had awakened him and attributed his feeling of peace to that. He repeated the line, "…and I commit him into Your hands." He didn't know exactly what it meant, but he thanked the Lord anyway.

Methuselah suddenly sat up in a daze, "Father, was I praying in my sleep?"

Enoch had to laugh, "I woke up doing the same thing." He waited before speaking again, "How do you feel about things this morning?"

Methuselah rubbed his eyes, "You know, I feel at peace about whatever happens today. It feels good. I haven't had that feeling in a few days."

Enoch nodded, "I do too. Whatever happens today, the Lord is with us." Methuselah nodded and stretched. Enoch lightened his mood, "So, let's have some breakfast. I am hungry!" Methuselah smiled and nodded again.

After a hearty breakfast of melon and bread, they packed up camp and prepared to reenter the city. While packing the last items into the carriage, they noticed a family walking somberly toward the city gates. Methuselah recognized them instantly, "Father, it's the family we met on the road when we were coming into the city yesterday."

Enoch looked and saw that he was right, "Yes, it is."

The two men stood beside the road and greeted them, "Hello again." The man only gave him a passing glance before looking back down to his feet as he continued on his forlorn way. His wife did not even look up. She only clutched her child closer as she whispered softly into his ear.

Enoch looked at his son and shrugged his shoulders. They then got into the carriage and followed them through the gates.

The city had a strange feel about it today, somehow stranger than before. There was no hustle and bustle. There was no bartering at the market. There was only silence as slow processions of people headed in the same direction. Enoch and Methuselah knew where they were all going; toward the furnace.

It was then that the two men realized why the couple who had entered the city gates before them was so sad. They were taking their child to be sacrificed. Methuselah looked at his father wide-eyed, "Father, we must not let them do it! They are going to hand their child over to Simyaza!"

Enoch's heart sank with the same recognition, "We will have to try and stop them!" Enoch could see them up ahead, but the crowds were getting thicker now, and they could not catch up with them in the bulky carriage without running someone over. "Methuselah, we will have to get out of the carriage to catch them." Methuselah agreed, and they pulled the carriage into a side street and hopped off.

By the time they did this, they had lost sight of the little family in the growing crowd. Methuselah jumped as high as he could but to no avail. "I do not see them!"

Enoch found the raised platform of an empty cart to stand on and scanned the scene. "I cannot see them either, but we know where they are going. We will have to find them there. Let's go!" They made their way through the slow-moving crowd as fast as they could but kept getting clogged in the bottlenecks of the winding streets. Eventually, Enoch found that he had lost sight of Methuselah too. However, he did not panic at this. He also knew where *he* was headed.

If no one was on the streets, or he did not know exactly where the furnace was, it would not have made any difference. Enoch could have just followed the stench that emanated from it in every direction. He eventually caught sight of the column of putrid black smoke that rose from the mouth of the atrocity itself. As he rounded the final corner, he saw a smiling Simyaza standing atop the furnace, happily watching all of his "children" making their way into the square to view the morbid happenings.

Enoch's soul was sickened by the sight, so he busied himself with looking for the young couple and his son in the increasingly growing mass of people. Try as he might, he could not find them. He looked in vain for something to stand on, but there was nothing, only flat, dusty ground. He finally resigned himself to his only option; prayer.

As he closed his eyes, he heard the voice of Simyaza holler out from his lofty perch above, "Welcome, my children! Welcome! We are gathered here together for a great purpose today. We have come to give our encouragement to your neighbors who have finally decided to allow me to bless them with the prosperity they deserve!"

Simyaza then looked down to the base of the furnace steps and curled his long, boney fingers, motioning that someone should come up to where he was. Enoch saw that the man and his wife slowly made their way up. He started pushing his way through the crowd toward the furnace as quickly as he could. He had to get closer if he was going to stop them. As he did so, he saw that the sad couple was now standing next to Simyaza, and the evil being began to speak again.

"People of Baalta, I welcome you today. We are all here to celebrate the inspiring faith of Dornos and his wife, who have decided to show their trust in me and my master, the true god of this world! It is with great joy that I welcome them into our family and ask you to do the same. My master and I are overjoyed that we can finally bless them as they make their precious sacrifice." Dornos and his wife did not even look at the crowd as they cheered. They only continued staring at the child they loved, the child they were about to give up in a perverted trade for their own prosperity.

Simyaza continued when the throng had settled again, "However, my children, I am going to offer a rather unusual option for them today." He paused at this point for dramatic effect. The crowd became very quiet. They had never heard of any "option," so they waited breathlessly to hear what it could be.

"In order to show that my master is merciful, he has decreed that a trade can be made. If there is a firstborn son in the crowd today, who is willing to offer himself in place of this little one, I will accept their sacrifice in his place. All the blessings for this substitute sacrifice will still be credited to the account of Dornos and his family." The crowd was silent, stunned by this new revelation.

Enoch also was stunned. He thought to himself, "What is Simyaza up to? What is he trying…" His thoughts were suddenly interrupted by a familiar voice from somewhere to his left.

"I will stand in the place of this child!"

Enoch's heart sank as he saw Methuselah making his way to the base of the stairway leading to the top of the furnace. He cried out to him, "Methuselah, no!"

Methuselah calmly walked over to him and embraced him tenderly, whispering in his ear, "Father, this was what I was dreaming about when we made camp at the lake on our way here. This is why the Lord had me come along on this trip. I know this is not what you want, but I am at peace about it. This is what the Lord wants me to do." With that, Methuselah kissed his father on the forehead and turned back toward the furnace.

Enoch watched helplessly as his son made his way up the stairs. His heart was breaking within his chest as tears streamed down his cheeks. He instinctively closed his eyes to pray. Suddenly, the words of the Creator began to flow through his mind; words from an earlier conversation in the arboretum of the king's residence, "You will know what to do when the time comes. Just remember, put your faith in Me. Do not rely on your own understanding. When it looks as though all hope is lost, My timing is perfect."

The words of the Lord washed over his troubled soul and left only peace in place of his fears. It would have been difficult, if not impossible, for anyone else to understand the peace he was now feeling in such a terrible situation, but Enoch had seen the Lord come to his rescue so many times before that he had learned to completely rest in His goodness. Enoch whispered a short prayer. "Lord, I trust You. You will provide a way."

He opened his eyes again and saw the young couple tearfully embracing Methuselah at the top of the furnace before quickly returning down the steps and through the crowd. It was easy to see that they would not waste any time in case Simyaza changed his mind.

Simyaza now eyed Methuselah with a satisfied smile. Methuselah only looked him directly in the eye, sternly staring him down. Simyaza seemed surprised by the lack of fear in the young man's eyes, "You *are* a brave one, aren't you?" Methuselah did not answer. He only continued the steady, fearless stare until Simyaza could not take it anymore and had to look away.

Simyaza cleared his throat and addressed the crowd again, "As you all know, I am not cruel in the way I accept these sacrifices. I do not take a child away from its parents unless that child is freely given. This is the only way that true faith in me can be accepted. Therefore, does this young man's father give him freely in complete faith in me and my master?"

Enoch was usually a meek sort of man. However, he himself was almost surprised by the solid and robust tones in which he now spoke. "I give you my son in place of the child of Dornos.

However, I do not give him to you to show any faith in you or your master! I give him in the name of the One True God of Creation, the God of my fathers! I do this freely to show that true faith does not require such an abominable sacrifice to a liar and a devil as you and your master!"

Enoch now turned and faced the crowd of stunned onlookers, "True faith in the True God does not require that you sacrifice the lives of your children. True faith is in living your lives in a way that honors God and shows appreciation for the *gift* of your children. It only requires that we show our love for the Creator by taking care of those gifts; nurturing those gifts; and raising those gifts—*your children*—in a way that instills that same kind of love in them. Do you not understand what you have been doing here? You have been killing your own children in order to gain so-called "blessings" from this *liar*! You have been trading the gifts that God has given you for illusions, lies, and promises of blessings that never really come."

Enoch made his way up the stairway a few steps to see the crowd better, "You people have been so deceived that you actually think you have been blessed when, in reality, you have cursed yourselves! You think that you have been worshiping Simyaza in order to gain his favor, but the truth is, you have been worshiping yourselves! Simyaza is only a representation of the selfishness in your own hearts. You sacrifice your precious children because you think it helps you. In reality, you do not want to be bothered with the responsibility of raising your children. It takes a different kind of sacrifice to raise children in a way that honors God. There are times when you have to deny yourself something in order to give your children what they need. Your children need your love, but you are too preoccupied with loving yourselves! You act as if you are devoted to this liar, but you are more devoted to your..."

"Enough!!" Simyaza screamed out. "I will not stand here and listen to any more of this blasphemy! I believe I have been more than lenient by letting him spew his poison. Those of you who have offered up your sacrifice can attest to the fact that you have received your blessings from me and my master. Is that not true?"

The crowd was silent. In fact, some of the people in the crowd were under conviction as a result of Enoch's words. With the Lord's help, he managed to pierce the blackness of some of their hearts and plant a seed of truth. The only sound that could be heard now was the tangible silence of those seeds growing. This silence visibly unnerved Simyaza as he shouted louder, "Is that not true?!" More silence.

Simyaza was now thoroughly enraged, like a spoiled child who suddenly found he was not getting his way. "Fine! I will show you all where your faith should lie! You heard this young man's father say that he freely gives him for sacrifice. Thus," Simyaza now looked to the sky and spoke to his master, "I commit this firstborn child into the hands of my master, the true god of this world!"

⸺◦✦◦⸺

Methuselah had been praying silently during this whole episode. His eyes had been shut the entire time as he recited from memory the times that the Lord had delivered him from certain harm in his young life. He now opened his eyes and looked down into the mouth of the furnace. There had been nothing but scorching heat and the putrid odor of countless abominations emanating from it so far. But, as he saw in his peripheral vision Simyaza circling around behind him, something else was starting to show through the blackness.

Time seemed to be slowing down for Methuselah. The further Simyaza got behind him, the slower time seemed to go. At the same moment, a bright, silvery-blue light began to emanate from somewhere deep in the bowels of the furnace. The further around him Simyaza walked, the brighter the light, which resembled beautiful blue flames, glowed. By the time Simyaza disappeared entirely from his view, no blackness could be seen at all. There was only this bright, comforting, cool, and love-filled blue flame that seemed to completely envelop Methuselah.

———◦◦◦◦———

Enoch watched painfully as Simyaza walked around behind his son and raised his foot, placing it directly in the small of Methuselah's back. Simyaza then grunted as he kicked his son over the edge with all the might and rage he could muster. Methuselah quickly disappeared from view without a sound. Enoch closed his eyes and stood there for a moment. It seemed that the sight he had just witnessed played over and over in his mind countless times. His heart sank a little more each time until a new feeling began to come over him.

———◦◦◦◦———

Methuselah felt as if he were being helped slowly and gently over the edge of the furnace platform and into the cool refreshing waters of a beautiful stream. As he floated down, the flames seemed to baptize him in pure love, pure comfort. All the worries and toils of his life just disappeared from his mind as they were replaced by joy and wellbeing.

At some point, he felt like he had stopped his descent into the baptismal flames and was now resting upon what seemed to be a cool, soft pillow. A sturdy yet quiet voice then spoke to him. He could not tell whether it spoke to his ears or his soul, but it washed over him in a cascade of delight, "Methuselah, you have shown great faith. Your faith will be rewarded. You shall live a full life with many joys and blessings. Through your bloodline, I will bless the world with a Savior. He will crush the head of the Evil One forever."

—◦⁄◦⁄◦—

The ground beneath Enoch began to quiver slightly. At first, he thought that perhaps his legs were failing him, but he was still upright. He opened his eyes and saw everyone in the crowd looking at the ground around them. He looked down too. The small pebbles on the ground by his feet started dancing upon the surface as the quivering grew to a full shaking. The people around him were beginning to wonder out loud about what was happening. This became a total panic as the shaking intensified, and the earth started to roar. Instinctively, the people dropped to the ground and sprawled out to steady themselves the best they could as they began bouncing up and down in the quaking.

Suddenly, there was an earsplitting "CRACK!" Then, as quickly as the tremors had begun, the earth stopped shaking. There air was filled with dust, making it hard to see anything as the people slowly started to stand and survey their surroundings. Enoch had also found himself on the ground and stood and looked toward the furnace. A bright, silvery-blue light seemed to shine through the dust cloud that obscured his view. As the dust slowly blew away, he could see that the base of the furnace had a broad, gaping crack down one side, the edges jagged, as if a huge egg had been split open and stood upright so you could see inside.

There, he could see the strange yet comforting light centered within. By now, the entire assembly had regained their composure and was staring into the same breach of the furnace wall, marveling at the same light. Then, two figures began to emerge from the shadow of the light.

—*◊◊◊*—

When the voice had finished speaking, Methuselah saw natural light, which looked dull and dank compared to the light he had been bathing in, begin to appear before him. It started high above him and proceeded to make its way down to the base, forming a jagged line and widening as it went. He heard the voice again. "Go back into your life. Remember, I will always be with you through the troubles that will come your way. Also, remember, the troubles of this life, no matter how great they may seem, are *nothing* compared to the blessings of the life to come." With that, he began moving forward into the day's dirty light.

—*◊◊◊*—

Methuselah floated slowly out. His form was drenched by the soothing flames, as if they were made of shimmering water, until he made his way past the shore of the furnace walls. The flames then seemed to roll off of him and release him into the natural daylight as if he were a stone being drawn out of a stream, and the water rolled off of it to reveal its surface, clean and fresh.

Behind him was the other figure. It had the shape of a man. However, it seemed to be made of an even brighter, whiter light than the silvery-blue flames. It was glorious in nature, yet awful at the same time. This light was almost tangible. It seemed to be made of pure love, yet it inspired fear due to its intense purity. One knew that they were utterly unworthy of its approach. The whole assembly fell once again to their knees. This time, they fell because of a shaking within instead of a shaking from without.

As the purer light made its way to the shoreline of the furnaces outer shell, it emerged just as Methuselah had. Yet, when it came into the natural light of day, it vanished and only left the blue, water-like fire to splash back into itself and disappear, leaving only the sorry sight of Baalta's exposed atrocities behind; fragments of bones; the tiny bones of Baalta's lost treasures.

—✦—

Simyaza knew that it was all over when the earth began shaking. He wasn't sure how or why, but his master's plan had been thwarted. If he was a mortal man, he would have fallen into the furnace's mouth. However, he had only to vanish into a whisp of smoke and reappear somewhere else to escape. He decided to watch the happenings from atop a nearby building.

He was horrified to see Methuselah walk unharmed out of the gaping wall of his precious furnace. Even more horrible was the sight of all his "children" on their knees in awe of the boy's miraculous resurrection from what should have been certain death. It was, in a sense, what he had always wanted to see. However, he wanted the people to be on their knees before himself. The sight sickened him to the point that he could take no more. He again vanished into a puff of putrescent, black smoke as he recited curses on the man, Enoch, and his son.

—✦—

Enoch raised his arms high in the air. He ran to his son, encompassing him in a forceful, viselike embrace that made Methuselah wince in pain due to its enthusiasm. "My son, I praise the Lord for your safety!"

Methuselah wriggled a bit to keep his father from breaking a rib in his excitement until Enoch finally eased his grasp. "Father, it was amazing! I cannot wait to tell you what happened! It was so wonderful!"

By this time, the people of Baalta had begun to surround them. Of course, they appeared curious about what had happened to Methuselah, but there was something else in their eyes; they were completely lost. Their lives had been turned upside down by Simyaza, but it was what they had come to accept. However, as they looked around for their governor, he could not be found. Now they were leaderless and had been beaten down by Simyaza's oppressive regime to the point that they also felt powerless. Enoch felt compassion for them as he looked around him and into their empty eyes.

One of the men found courage and spoke to Enoch through the tears of awakening, "I know that you were right in what you said about us. You must think that we are monsters for allowing those things to happen. Now that you have opened our eyes to what we have become, I see *myself* as a monster. I forced my own wife into handing our son over to Simyaza! I'm not even sure how it happened."

Enoch walked over and put a comforting hand on the man's shoulder. "Sir, the enemy of your soul is very adept at what he does. He is very cunning. He takes the things that God has put in place and distorts them. He makes a cheap counterfeit that is designed to fool you into thinking that you are doing the right things when, in reality, you are doing the complete opposite. But what you need to realize is that Simyaza had no real power of his own. He only had the power that you gave him. He had no authority in your lives until you began to believe the lies he told about himself. His power was nothing more than an illusion."

The man's eyes filled with tears as he asked his next question, "Can God ever forgive me for what I have done?"

Enoch smiled at him and all the others that surrounded them. In a strong voice, he answered, "Yes, He can!"

———✺———

At the far end of the square, Jeru and Ronin looked on as their entire reason for being in Baalta crumbled away. The two men exchanged a knowing glance and slinked away quietly out of the city with their wolves in tow. There was no life for them here any longer.

Chapter 23

*I*T WAS MIDDAY AT THE KING'S RESIDENCE, AND THE courtyard was beginning to take on quite a festive look. Brightly dyed purple, white, and red silken cloths were tied together and stretched from lamp post to lamp post, atop which large flames were burning to bathe the entire courtyard in light deep into the night. Everyone was busy with one chore or another as they prepared to have a celebration in honor of Analeah's homecoming to faith.

Tamari was finding it therapeutic to busy her hands with something other than wringing them and worrying about Methuselah. She missed him terribly and longed so much to see him riding back into the Royal City. In this effort, she had spent a large portion of the day learning how to carve pieces of fruit in such a way that they looked like flowers. She had trouble initially but was starting to get the hang of it. As her father walked by carrying one end of a heavy wooden bench, she shoved it up to his face excitedly, "Look, Father! Look what I have learned to do today! It's a flower made of two kinds of melon. Isn't it pretty?"

Jaylon had to stop suddenly, dropping his end of the table, and back away from it a bit to get it into focus as it had been shoved so close to his nose that he thought Tamari might shove it right into his nostrils. He was a bit confused as to how exactly what she was holding looked anything like a flower, but upon hearing the excitement of her accomplishment in her voice, he had no choice but to answer, "That *is* beautiful Tamari. You have shown a real talent there."

Tamari bounced a bit at the compliment, "Thank you, Father. I think it looks pretty good too."

At that moment, Julis was walking by carrying a platter with fresh sweet breads and added her input, "It doesn't look like a flower to me."

Tamari gave her a playful scowl as she retorted, "I would like to see you do better."

She watched as Julis only shrugged her shoulders and raised her eyebrows as if to say, "I bet I could." But her attention was taken by something behind her. It was a carriage coming around the corner of the king's residence.

Tamari could not contain herself as she recognized the two men in the carriage, "Methuselah!" She ran as fast as she could to close the gap between them. Methuselah stood and smiled as big as he could when he saw his soon-to-be bride running his way. He leaped out of the still-moving carriage and raced toward her. By now, the entire entourage had stopped what they were doing and watched as the young couple finally reached each other.

Methuselah wrapped his arms around her, bringing her off her feet as he spun her around. Tamari squealed in delight as always when he did that, and she began kissing his neck in rapid procession. The men looked on, a bit embarrassed by the overdone show of emotion on display before them. The women looked on longingly as they thought about the days when their own husbands would carry on that way without regard for who was watching.

However, Julis looked on, shaking her head. She spoke to Jubal, standing beside her, "Can you believe those two? They are shameless!" She did not get a verbal response and turned to see if Jubal had been listening at all. Upon turning, she found herself face to face with the young man she loved. He looked deeply at her and kissed her with authority. She did not generally like big shows of emotion, but as he released her and continued to look at her lovingly, she was undone. She turned and melted back against him, allowing his strong arms to envelop her.

He whispered into her ear softly, "I love *you* like that." The two contentedly watched as Methuselah and Tamari continued to celebrate their reunion. In the foreground, a bit more understated but no less powerful, another set of lovers met in an embrace to celebrate their own reunion. Enoch and Ednah just quietly held each other, unashamed and unapologetic about their show of affection.

Eventually, everyone had their chance to greet the returning heroes and hear the stories about the trip. They all praised the Lord for Methuselah's deliverance and were glad to add that to the many other reasons for the celebration.

The party went on deep into the night. Analeah was feeling great about all the new friends she had made here in the Royal City but was missing the one in particular that she wanted to celebrate with the most. As the night went on, she resigned herself to the fact that Mother Eve would not make it.

Some of the people had started to make their way home or back into the king's residence. After all, there was a wedding tomorrow, and many preparations still had to be made. Analeah yawned and stretched. That was her signal. She had had enough excitement for the day and was going to bed. She said goodnight to many of the people as she headed toward the doors.

She was almost there when she heard the clip-clop of horses' hooves on the city's streets. She turned to see who it was, hoping to see Father Adam and Mother Eve riding into the square. At first, she thought it was someone else since there were four people in the approaching carriage. However, as they got closer, her heart nearly jumped out of her chest.

Analeah squealed with delight. Not only was it Father Adam and Mother Eve. They had brought her real mother and father with them. She ran and met them as they got down from the carriage, and the little family fell into each other's arms, sobbing loudly and kissing each other.

Father Adam and Mother Eve quietly made their way down and around to where King Seth was standing and watching the reunion. He spoke first, "I see you were right, Mother. That is *exactly* what she needed."

Eve only smiled and spoke softly to her son, "I would be surprised to find that you did not realize, a hurting child sometimes just needs her mother."

Analeah had spent a long time speaking with her parents. Many embraces and tears were exchanged until Father Adam showed them to a room where they could rest from a long day's journey. Analeah was now alone in the courtyard, thinking about what the last few days had meant to her.

She had made new friends. She had met the Mother of all Humanity. She had met a giant and his behemoth and found him to be more genuine than most of the people she had ever had in her life. She had been allowed to find redemption from sins she thought could never be forgiven. And she had been reunited with the parents she hadn't seen in more than four years.

—◦◦◦—

Gardan had watched the celebration from a safe distance away most of the evening. Many people had come by and spoken with him but could detect a somber mood in the normally jovial giant. The truth was that he was feeling a bit sad about something he wanted but knew he could probably never have; the true love of a woman of his own kind.

Over the last few days, he had become keenly aware for the first time that he was capable of being intimately attracted to a woman. The rub lay in the fact that the woman with which he was smitten was already married. Even worse, she was married to a man he felt did not deserve her.

Therefore, he chose to sit back in the shadows and watch Analeah dance, celebrate, smile, laugh, and enjoy her new-found freedom. All the while, Gardan was becoming more aware of the prison walls erecting themselves around his newly broken heart. He silently prayed, "Lord, will I ever have *that* kind of love for myself? You have made it possible for me to feel so many kinds of love. Is this the one love that is forbidden to me?"

—◦◦◦—

Analeah's heart felt so glad for all the wonderful things she had experienced, but something was still missing. She sat quietly, looking up at the stars pondering all this, alone in the now silent courtyard, when the sound of footsteps jarred her from her thoughts. She looked down and saw the last person she thought she would see this night.

Her voice cracked slightly as she said, "Jotham!" The man she had spent what seemed like an eternity hating was there before her. He stood there silently, just staring at her. She wanted to yell at him, hit him, and threaten his life if he did not leave. But there was something different about him. He did not look like the man she had hated all this time. He looked like a sad, lost, and broken man. She just stared back at him. She stood to turn and leave him standing there, but she couldn't. Her legs would not move. She watched as the shell of a man sank to his knees before her and sobbed at her feet. She wanted to kick him. She could not. Her mind wanted anything but what her heart was telling her.

A voice within her was saying something she did not want to hear. She tried desperately to ignore it, but it just kept repeating the same thing over and over, "You have been forgiven so much. What right do *you* have not to do the same for him?"

She finally gave in and fell to her knees to look Jotham in the eyes. When their eyes met, the hatred seemed to melt away. She felt love for her husband again for the first time in a long time. She was not ready to say it yet, but the fact that she felt it was enough for now.

Gardan had seen the whole episode from the shadows. A giant tear fell from his eye as he sat and watched the last remaining whisp of hope vanish before him. He knew it was only a fantasy. However, even fantasies can be comforting while you are in them. When they are over, only emptiness remains.

———✦———

The courtyard was quiet and solemn, save for the songbirds singing their melodies to the day. Methuselah stood looking at the main doors leading out of the king's residence. It felt as if he were standing there forever. The doors finally opened. On her father's arm was the most beautiful sight he had ever seen. As their eyes met, he melted again, just as he had done every day since he had met her.

As they approached the altar, Jaylon took his daughter's hand in his and kissed it. He then took hold of Methuselah's hand and placed the two hands together. Jaylon then spoke loudly and clearly for all to hear, "In the sight of God and all these witnesses, I freely give my daughter in marriage." He then turned and went to his seat as he wiped a happy tear from his eye.

The rest of the day was spent in celebration. There were gifts given and music and dancing. Wonderfully large and elaborate tables of every variety of food were consumed as laughter and happiness filled the courtyard. All the women wore different flowers from Tara's garden in their hair and soaked in the loving atmosphere that always accompanied a wedding, an atmosphere that seemed to engender an attempt at courtship by their respective husbands who had, perhaps, had their passions cooled with age.

Analeah and Jotham sat quietly at a table together. They would sometimes talk. At other times, no words were exchanged at all. Analeah could not remember feeling more awkward. Thankfully, the awkwardness was broken up occasionally by the wonderfully refreshing sight of her mother and father dancing together as if they were young lovers again. She knew that her relationship with Jotham would probably never be the same as before, but she at least felt that there was hope for a new one now.

Gardan had been present for the wedding and for much of the celebration. He had congratulated Methuselah and Tamari wholeheartedly. He was truly happy for them. However, his heart was feeling something he was not used to feeling; jealousy. The more he watched the new couple, the more he felt this new and unwelcome emotion.

To make matters worse, Analeah seemed to be completely ignoring him now and spending all her time with her husband. He knew that it didn't really matter in the end. He and Analeah could never have had a future together. But knowing that did not make the pain any less real. He could not endure more torture and quietly slipped away from the party and out of the city. He needed to be alone, just he and Nahla.

Enoch knew Gardan better than anyone. He also knew that something was bothering him but decided, for now at least, to let him work it out himself. He watched as his enormous friend disappeared from sight with his head bowed in sadness and prayed for him, "Lord, I pray your comfort and mercy on Gardan."

To order additional copies of

Passing Through the Fire;
The Methuselah Chronicles

Book Two

visit www.amazon.com